The Love of a Rogue

HEART OF A DUKE SERIES

CHRISTI CALDWELL

SPENCER
HILL
PRESS

Please visit www.christicaldwellauthor.com

First Edition: March 2015
Christi Caldwell

The Love of a Rogue: a novel / by Christi Caldwell—1st ed.
ISBN: 978-1-63392-105-4
Library of Congress Cataloging-in-Publication Data available upon request

Summary: Lady Imogen Moore hasn't had an easy time of it since she made her
Come Out three Seasons ago. With her betrothed, a powerful duke, breaking it off to
wed her sister, she's become the *ton*'s favorite piece of gossip. Never again wanting
to experience the pain of a broken heart, she's resolved to make a match with a
polite, respectable gentleman. The last thing she wants is another reckless rogue.

Lord Alex Edgerton has a problem. His brother, tired of Alex's carousing, has
charged him with chaperoning their remaining, unwed sister about *ton* events.
He'd rather be at Forbidden Pleasures with a scantily clad beauty upon his lap. The
task of chaperone becomes even more of a bother when his sister drags along her
dearest friend, Lady Imogen, to social functions.

Except, as Alex and Imogen are thrown together, passions flare and Alex
comes to find he not only wants Imogen in his bed, but also in his heart. Yet now
he must convince Imogen to risk all, on the heart of a rogue.

Published in the United States by Spencer Hill Press.
This is a Spencer Hill Press Contemporary Romance.
Spencer Hill Contemporary is an imprint of Spencer Hill Press.
For more information on our titles, visit www.spencerhillpress.com

Distributed by Midpoint Trade Books
www.midpointtrade.com

Cover Design by: The Killion Group, Inc.
Interior layout by: Scribe Inc.

Printed in the United States of America

Heart of a Duke Series

WE ALL NEED A LITTLE HELP IN MAKING OUR DREAMS COME TRUE.

To Dr. Leondires, Dr. Patrizio, Dr. Fleischman, and Dr. Reel for allowing me my first dream—the dream of becoming a mother.

AND TO MY AMAZING READERS

Every day you allow me my second dream—turning out worlds of happily-ever-afters—and for that, I thank you.

I'm nothing without you.

Contents

Chapter 1

London, England
1815

$\mathcal{T}$he day Lady Imogen Isabel Moore had made her Come Out almost three Seasons ago, she'd taken the *ton* by storm.

Not, however for any reasons that were good.

One glass of lemonade held in trembling fingers, one graceless misstep, and an inconveniently situated Lady Jersey in the hallowed halls of Almack's had placed Imogen in polite Society's focus. At the time, that moment with the glass of lemonade had proven the most disastrous of her then eighteen years. In a single night, she'd shocked polite Society . . . and also earned the attention of the gloriously handsome William, the Duke of Montrose.

With a sigh, Imogen glanced down at the copy of *The Times.*

The D of M, recently wedded, had returned to London . . .

She skimmed the details of the article. *Hopelessly in love. Devoted . . . Love at any cost . . .* Imogen tossed the newspaper aside, where it landed with a thump upon the mahogany side table.

He'd returned. The gloriously handsome golden duke with his glib tongue and winning smile and his black heart. And he'd returned with his wife—Imogen's, younger by a year sister, Rosalind. Or, the Duchess of Montrose, as she was now properly titled.

"Never tell me you are melancholy again."

A gasp escaped her and she spun around so quickly, a blindingly bright, crimson curl slipped free of its chignon and tumbled over her eye. In a flurry of noisy, blue bombazine skirts, her mother swept into the room. "Mother," Imogen greeted with a weak smile for the parent who'd merely been happy that one of her daughters had secured the duke's title. None of the rest had mattered. "I'm not melancholy," she added as an afterthought. Egad. Her lips pulled in a grimace. That faithless, roguish duke she'd imagined herself in love with had turned her into one of those dreadfully miserable types to be around.

Mother came to a stop before her and wordlessly brushed the errant, hideously red curl back behind Imogen's ear. Narrowing her eyes like a doddering lord in need of his monocle, she peered at Imogen.

Imogen drew back. "What is it?"

"I'm looking for tears. There are to be no tears. Your sister is happy and that should bring you happiness and . . ." Her mother launched into a familiar lecture; a nonsensical lesson on sibling loyalty expected of Imogen when her own sister had been anything but. ". . . you will take the *ton* by storm." Those hopeful words brought her to the moment.

An inelegant snort escaped her, earning a hard frown from her mama. "I did take the *ton* by storm, Mother. Remember? There was the whole incident with the lemonade two," nearly three, "years ago." That defining moment that had brought the Duke of Montrose into her life and into her heart.

That blasted glass of lemonade.

Her mother waved a hand about. "Oh, do hush, Imogen. That is not the manner of storm to which I refer." Alas,

Mother had never been capable of detecting sarcasm. "You shall go to events and smile and find a gentleman."

"I found a gentleman," she took an unholy joy in pointing out. "The Du—"

"Would you have had him wed where his heart was not engaged?" That handful of words struck like a well-placed barb.

Ah, so her mother had become something of a romantic. "Indeed, not," she squeezed out past tight lips. Greed for a duke tended to do that to a title-grasping mama.

"We shall find you a powerful, titled nobleman and then you shall be blissfully happy. Just as your sister." Another well-placed mark. If her mother weren't so very flighty, Imogen would have believed her words were intended with deliberate cruelty. A startled squeak escaped her as her mother claimed her cheeks in her hands and squished Imogen's face. "I promise this shall be your last Season as an unwed lady. We shall see you attend all the most popular events and dance with all the most eligible bachelors." All of which sounded utterly dreadful. With a smile, her mother released Imogen and spun on her heel.

Her mind raced. Surely even her flighty mother knew that anything and everything the *ton* discussed would not be Imogen's suitability as a match, but the scandal surrounding her name. "But—" Her protestation trailed off as her mother slipped from the room. From the corner of her eye, the open copy of *The Times* stared mockingly at her. With a curse unfit for most gentlemen's ears, she swiped the newspaper and carried it over to the window seat. As she claimed a seat, Imogen scoured the page for other poor souls who'd already earned the *ton*'s attention this Season.

Lord AE, the notorious Lord Alexander Edgerton, has taken up residence at his scandalous clubs and gaming hells.

Well, that was hardly news. She scoffed. Lord Alexander Edgerton, her dearest friend Chloe's brother, had earned a reputation as quite the scapegrace. A rogue. A scoundrel. In short, another Duke of Montrose.

The young duke had, at one time, been an outrageous, scandalous gentleman most mamas would turn their noses up at. Until a distant relative had gone and died making him the unlikely new duke . . . and suddenly perfect marriageable material for all those protective mamas.

Imogen threw the paper aside once again and turned her attention to the window, studying the passersby below. There were certainly worse things than having your betrothed sever the contract just three days before the blessed wedding. It was a good deal harder finding those worse things when one's betrothed broke your engagement—to marry your sister. Imogen desperately tried to call up those worse things.

She could . . .

Or there was . . .

Imogen sighed. Nothing. There was surely nothing worse than this.

A soft rapping at the door cut into her musings.

Imogen knocked her head against the wall. "Go away," she murmured to herself. She didn't want company. Certainly not her harebrained mother. Another knock. She was content to become one of those outrageous spinsters who brought their wildly attired pups to fashionable events and earned furious amounts of stares from—

Another knock. "My lady . . ."

Oh, bother. "Do come in," she bit out, not taking her gaze from the carriages rattling along the London streets below.

The butler cleared his throat. "Lady Chloe Edgerton to see you."

Imogen spun about. Her best friend stood in the doorway, a wry smile on her pretty face.

Imogen dangled her legs over the side of the seat. "Chloe," she greeted with far more excitement than she'd felt for anything or anyone since the broken betrothal. She'd been wrong. There was one person she'd care to see.

"Imogen." Chloe swung her reticule back and forth.

The butler discreetly backed out of the room and pulled the door quietly closed.

"I gather you've heard the news," Imogen said without preamble. She'd never been one to prevaricate.

Chloe tipped her head. "The news?" She tapped her hand to the center of her forehead once. "Ah, yes, silly me. Did you mean about Lord Whetmore's horse nipping Lady McTavishs's shoulder? Quite scandalous really."

Imogen appreciated what her friend was doing. She really did. Her shoulders sank and she returned her attention to the window. It was hard to be happy when your sister had so betrayed you and your betrothed had humiliated you. Even a best friend who'd boldly challenged all your nasty enemies at finishing school didn't have much of a chance in rousing you from your melancholy.

Chloe sank beside her in a flutter of ivory skirts. "I do hate seeing you like this," she said quietly, setting aside her matching ivory reticule.

Imogen mustered a wan smile. "And I hate being like this." Nobody preferred a gloomy, despondent creature. Then again, her betrothed clearly hadn't preferred her happy and loquacious. So really, who knew what one wanted, after all?

A dandy in garish, canary-yellow knee breeches and a lady in like color chose that awful, inopportune moment to glance up. The couple in the street widened their eyes and stared openly at her.

Chloe reached over and drew the curtain completely closed. "Busybodies," she mumbled.

With a scandal was as great as Imogen's, even the rare few who didn't partake in gossip now bandied her name about.

"It will get better," her friend said with a confidence Imogen didn't feel. She leaned over and patted her hand. "Why, I daresay you are better off without one such as him."

"Polite Society does not agree," Imogen said, a wry smile on her lips. With his golden-blond Brutus curls and his grinning countenance, the Duke of Montrose's company was desired by all—including her sister.

Chloe squeezed her hands. "Look at me."

Imogen lifted her gaze.

"You are better off without him." Chloe wrinkled her nose. "Why, I heard Mama say he's quite a rogue and not at all proper."

Yes, breaking a formal arrangement to wed your betrothed's younger sister certainly spoke to that truth. Imogen curled her hands into tight fists. Though for one considered to be a rogue, he'd hardly demonstrated an amorous intention toward Imogen. Embarrassment turned in her belly.

"You wouldn't want to marry him. Not when he's proven himself inconstant. You deserve more than that." Chloe paused and when next she spoke, she did so in hushed tones. "Don't you remember what you confessed at Mrs. Belton's?"

Ah, yes, Mrs. Belton would not be pleased by this very public shaming of one of her students. For purely self-serving reasons, of course. After all, a headmistress's reputation was bound to the ladies she turned out into the world.

Chloe nudged her in the side.

Imogen grunted. "Love. I said I'd wanted to make a love match." She'd believed she loved William and, worse, believed he'd loved her, too. What a naïve fool she'd been. A young girl so desperate for that emotion in her life, she'd convinced herself of foolish dreams. And yet, a shameful, pathetic sliver of her soul still longed for that dangerous, painful emotion.

"You do remember." A wide smile wreathed her friend's face. "Splendid." Chloe glanced about, as though searching for interlopers. She reached for her reticule and fished around inside the elaborate, satin piece. "I've brought you something," she said, dropping her voice to a conspiratorial whisper.

The faintest stirring of curiosity filled Imogen; any sentiment beyond the self-pitying, pained fury she carried was a welcome emotion. Chloe withdrew a shining gold chain. The sun's morning rays filtered through the crack in the curtains and played off the small heart pendant. Imogen studied the light reflecting off the glimmering heart. "It is beautiful," she murmured.

"Here, take it," Chloe prodded. She pressed it into Imogen's fingers. "It is yours."

"I couldn't." Imogen made to push it back.

"It belonged to Lady Anne, the Countess of Stanhope."

Imogen blinked several times. "What?" she blurted. The young lady, courted by the powerful Duke of Crawford, then betrothed to her cousin, had quite scandalized the *ton* when she'd abruptly ended her engagement and wed the roguish Earl of Stanhope. In fact, it had been the last scandal to shock the *ton* . . . until Imogen. "How?" She couldn't string together a coherent thought. The faint stirrings of unease rolled through her. Oh, dear she didn't care to know the extent her friend had gone to obtain the piece.

"Lady Anne is married to Alex's closest friend, Lord Stanhope. It was nothing to speak to the woman."

Oh, please let the floor open up and swallow me whole. "You didn't." She dropped her head into her hands and shook it back and forth.

"I did." Chloe nodded excitedly. "You see," she spoke in such hushed tones, it brought Imogen's head up. "The necklace," she nodded to it, "is the same one worn by her sisters and a handful of their friends. It is fabled to land the wearer the heart of a duke and as you've already had a duke, you'd instead want one of those noblemen, but this time, his heart as—"

Oh, please, no. "You did not speak to her." Shame curled Imogen's toes.

Chloe paused, mouth opened, thought unfinished, only confirming Imogen's suspicions. "She was entirely gracious." Imogen winced. "And understanding." She flinched again. "And more than happy to gift you the heart pendant." Chloe wrinkled her brow. "Or rather, give me the pendant to pass along to you." An uncharacteristically somber light filled her dearest friend's eyes. "I just want you to be happy once more."

So much so that she'd unknowingly humiliate Imogen before a stranger. Imogen sighed, not knowing if she should laugh or cry.

Chloe claimed her hands and gave them a squeeze. "You will find the gentleman who is your true love. I promise." Through the years, Chloe had been the more practical, logical of them when it came to matters of the heart, swearing off that emotion for herself while allowing, even supporting, Imogen in that dream.

Imogen hardly recognized this young woman who spoke of magic and pendants and dreams of love. With a sound of impatience, she shoved to her feet, her fist tightened reflexively about the chain. "This is about more than love." Imogen began to pace. Chloe had never been accused of being a hopeless romantic. Unlike Imogen—or rather, like Imogen had been, until life happened and showed her the folly in giving her heart to another. She increased her frantic movements. "It is about being respected, inspiring devotion, and dedication in another." Feats she'd failed miserably at where the Duke of Montrose was concerned.

Her friend hopped up and placed herself in Imogen's path. And then she said the only two words Imogen had longed to hear since the whole public shaming heaped on her by her disloyal sister and fickle betrothed. "I'm sorry," Chloe said softly.

That was it. Imogen just wanted someone to not make excuses or worry after the scandal and how Society looked on it. She wanted someone to care about her and that she'd been hurt.

Imogen mustered a smile. "He did have fetid breath."

A sharp bark of unexpected laughter bubbled past her friend's lips. "And he was entirely too tall." She shuddered. "We shan't find you a tall gentleman like him."

"And handsome," Imogen supplied, feeling vastly better for her friend's devoted teasing. "He was too handsome." Which is why her grasping, self-centered sister had first noticed him. The familiar stirring of fury turned in her belly. And she embraced it, far preferring it to the kicked and wounded pup she'd been since the unhappy occasion.

Determined to set aside the still fresh betrayal, Imogen threw herself back into her friend's game. "He drinks too much brandy." His breath had stunk of it whenever he was near. "I shan't ever wed a gentleman who touches even one glass of liquor."

"Splendid." Chloe gave a pleased nod. "You are quite grasping the spirit of this." She lowered her voice. "I've heard from my brother that His Grace has a wicked penchant for the gaming tables."

Imogen had little doubt just which brother Chloe spoke of. Not the respectable Marquess of Waverly but rather Lord Alex Edgerton, known rogue, skirt-chaser, reprobate, brandy drinker. Another gentleman all ladies would be best served to avoid.

Chloe clapped her hands once, jerking Imogen's attention back to her. "You're woeful again." A stern frown turned her lips down in the corners. "You must focus on how horrid and horrible and all things awful he is."

"Er. Yes, right." Except she'd run out of insulting charges to level on his miserable head. She stopped pacing so quickly, her satin skirts fluttered about her ankles. Though in truth, as hurt and humiliated as she was by his betrayal, she truly was better knowing the man's true character before she'd gone and wed him.

"I have an idea," her friend put in tentatively, which was all show. There was nothing tentative about Lady Chloe Edgerton.

"Oh?" Imogen asked dryly. Too many troublesome scrapes at Mrs. Belton's Finishing School had begun with those four words.

Chloe beamed with Imogen's interest. "Now that you have this necklace," she gestured to the chain in Imogen's hand, "you shall find a gentleman. And make him fall hopelessly and helplessly in love with you and His Grace will be outrageously, wickedly jealous."

"That is your plan?" She'd long adored her friend for her cleverness, however, this was an ill-thought-out idea on the lady's part. What was the use in making William jealous? "That will not change anything where Montrose is concerned."

Her friend plucked the necklace from her fingers. "Nor should you want to change anything, silly," Chloe murmured. "Here, turn around." Before Imogen could protest, Chloe spun her about. She settled the chain about her friend's neck and fiddled with the clasp. A soft click filled the quiet. "There," she said, turning Imogen around once more. "I'll have you know," she gave a toss of her blonde curls, "that was not my plan." A slow, mischievous grin turned her lips. "You rejoining Society was . . . is," she amended, "my plan."

Imogen had retreated from *ton* events after The Scandal, as Society had taken to referring to it. Those drawn out syllables the *ton* used to set it apart from other scandals. Imogen sighed. "I've little interest in entering Society." Alas, now that Rosalind had wed her duke, Mother's wedding plans were at an end, and she'd turned her sights once more upon Imogen. "I intend to wait until the scandal isn't so—"

Her friend's snort cut across the remainder of those hopeful words. "Oh, Imogen," she said gently, taking her friend's hands once more. "This scandal shall remain until some other foul lord goes and does something outrageous that captures their notice. I shan't allow you to bury your head in shame. Not when you haven't done anything wrong." Fire snapped in her blue eyes. "Is that clear?" Imogen opened her mouth to respond but Chloe gave a pleased nod. "We shall fill your days! There will be shopping trips and we'll take in the theater, and various balls . . ."

As her friend prattled on, Imogen groaned. All those options were about as appealing as being tasked with plucking out each strand of hair on her head, but most particularly any visits to Drury Lane. "Not the theater." There she would be on public display like one of those Captain Cook exhibits at the Egyptian Hall. She was brave. She was not that brave.

"You'll have me," her friend said, accurately interpreting her concerns. "The sooner you make your appearance and show the *ton* you'll not be cowed or shamed by them and miserable Montrose, then the sooner they shall move on to some other poor creature."

Imogen shot her a look.

Chloe had the good grace to blush. "Er . . . not that you're a poor creature."

Imogen tapped a finger to her lips. Insult aside, if she was being honest, it really wasn't an altogether awful plan. In fact, it was quite a brilliant one.

As though sensing victory was close, Chloe added, "Furthermore you'll be spared your mother's matchmaking for the Season."

Yes, Mother had begun to speak of the Marquess of Waverly with an increasing frequency. After all, by Mother's thinking, if one couldn't have a duke, she may as well aspire to a marquess. "Very well, I shall go." After all, the alternative would be to flit from one event to the next with her married sister and her beaming mother and the faithless Duke of Montrose for company.

"Splendid!" Chloe said, with a clap of her hands. "My brother Gabriel will accompany us. No one will dare slight you with the fierce Marquess of Waverly at our side."

Envy tugged at Imogen. Through the years, her own sister had been at best rude and condescending, and at worst, deliberately cruel, mocking the flame-red curls Imogen had been cursed with. She would have traded her left index finger to know the loving friendship Chloe had with her siblings.

With an energized stride, her friend started for the door. She paused at the threshold and spun back once more to face Imogen. "Prepare yourself, Imogen Moore. You are going to take Society by storm."

Not again.

Chapter 2

*T*he Marquess of Waverly steepled his fingers together, then folded them under his chin.

Lord Alex Edgerton, second son, spare to the heir, kicked his legs out and propped them on the edge of his brother's, the current marquess's, desk. "You summoned me?" He yawned and with his gaze sought the time from the long-case clock. Ungodly hour for a man to be awake.

Gabriel frowned and leaned forward in his chair. "I summoned you a week ago."

Had it been a week? Alex had thought the missive had arrived at his club two days past, but certainly not a week. Regardless . . . "I've been quite busy." He'd had a rotten run at the faro tables but some delicious company at Forbidden Pleasures.

"Busy?" His brother repeated in that incredulous, more than a little condescending tone. "What? At your whist tables?"

Alex bristled. "Hardly." Everyone knew he far preferred faro to whist. How disappointing that his brother, who knew everything, should fail to know this important detail about him.

"Then what?"

Alex blinked.

His brother lowered his voice in that reproachful, father-like manner of his. "Are you in such a liquor-induced stupor that you require my clarification?" Oh bloody hell. His brother was in a foul temper. "Very well," Gabriel continued, no prodding required from Alex. "Have you been too busy gaming and whoring and drinking to respond to a missive?"

"A summons."

His stodgy brother cocked his head.

Alex shifted, and knowing it would infuriate him, hooked his ankle over the other. "Yours was not a note. It was a summons. You are quite adept at ordering one about." He steeled his jaw. "Much like Father, you know. He'd be proud." Those deliberately needling words had the desired effect. His brother's eyes became thin slits and rage dripped from his frame.

How neatly Gabriel had slid into that detested role. Alex had been well and truly glad the day his miserable, violent sire had departed to the hereafter, never daring to imagine that Gabriel would become . . . *this*.

"Are we done here?" Alex asked, with another yawn. "If you remember, I mentioned I have important business to attend to." Particularly a lush brunette and a delectable blonde at Forbidden Pleasures who'd been quite inventive and eager last evening.

Gabriel sat back in his seat and folded his arms across his chest. "You've been losing at whist."

Faro. He'd had a deuced run of rotten luck. Alex sighed. "My luck always turns."

"The only thing turning with predictable frequency is your pockets; inside out as you squander away this family's fortune."

"My allowance," he felt inclined to point out. Every shilling of his allowance was a payment owed him for the lash of his father's birch rod. "I earned that," he whispered, not knowing he'd spoken aloud.

Gabriel scoffed. "You've never earned anything in your life. You've never worked for anything or known toil."

A dull heat climbed his neck at the charge that hit too close to the mark. "As opposed to your very diligent, prideful work?" He arched a taunting eyebrow at the other man, who, by his birthright, was entitled to anything and everything with no consideration of work.

Alas, his brother had grown immune to his baiting over the years. "I also don't squander away the gift given me as a nobleman's son." Gabriel had, however, become more precise with landing those pointed barbs. "Which brings me to the reason for my missive."

"Summons," Alex supplied.

A mottled flush stained his brother's face. "I'm cutting you off," he said at last.

Alex slid his legs off the edge of the desk and the heels of his boots scraped along the floor. "What was that?" He really shouldn't have had that bottle of brandy last evening. Fine French spirits, some of the best, but still he shouldn't have had quite so much. For it had sounded as though his brother had said—

"I'm cutting you off," Gabriel repeated with infuriating composure. He slashed his hand. "No allowance. Let to the pocket. Off at the knees." He grinned, a hard, cold smile. In that moment, Gabriel's face shifted and Alex now sat before the old marquess. Cold, heartless, grinning a vile black smile and reaching for that birch.

And even at twenty-nine years, Alex's mouth went dry with the familiar terror. He blinked, desperately longing for that fine French brandy now, for altogether different reasons.

"Nothing to say?" his brother drawled.

When had Gabriel become this methodical bastard? He'd really be quite impressed if Gabriel's ire wasn't even now turned on him. "I don't expect you're looking for a thank you." He said it with a half-grin, even as worry filled his belly with knots. He was completely and totally dependent upon that damned allowance—the one thing given him by his father. Of course, the evil bastard, even in death, had a wicked sense of humor by giving Alex's elder brother ultimate control over the younger, less revered son.

"Is everything a game to you? Your legions of mistresses." Hardly legions. Never more than one at a time. All in bad form. "Your debts at the gaming tables." He'd had a rotten run of luck. That was all there was to it. Gabriel ran a disgusted stare up and down his frame. "Tell me this. If you can provide one suitable, sufficient answer, I shall leave your allowance untouched and yours forever."

Alex braced.

"In your twenty-nine years, who have you loved more than yourself?"

He clenched and relaxed his jaw, unable to meet Gabriel's gaze and shamed by that unwitting weakness on his part. There had been a time when he'd loved Gabriel in that way, his older brother and champion who'd bravely stepped in and taken lashes meant for the younger failure of a brother. He loved his sisters now. And that was it. He firmed his lips, content to allow Gabriel his opinions. For Chloe and Philippa, he'd lay down his life.

The rest of the world could go hang. All Society likely saw was a self-absorbed, shallow figure of a man. Those people, his brother included, failed to look closely enough to see he cared for those deserving of his love and loyalty.

"No answer?" Gabriel peered down the length of his aquiline nose. "I am, of course, not surprised with your silence." He pinched the bridge of that same nose. "I've thought a good deal about what to do with you."

Alex steeled his jaw. His brother spoke of him as though he were a stray cat taken in by Cook, wreaking havoc on the kitchens. "There is nothing to be done," he said, his first defense of himself. "The money is mine." Alas, his hot temper had never been a boon to him.

"Ah, yes, it should be," Gabriel, said with entirely too much glee. "And it will."

Alex probed his brother with a hard stare. He'd learned long ago not to trust. Anyone or anything. Father had doled out plenty of lessons to school him in that particular point. Regardless, he'd tired of his brother's games. "Then I imagine we are done here." He shoved back his chair.

"You are to earn your allowance."

He froze half out of his chair and then reclaimed his seat. "I beg your pardon?" He gritted the question out past clenched teeth.

"Earn," his brother carried on. "As in work to acquire something. It comes as no surprise that you should fail to grasp the meaning of that important word."

Alex gripped the leather arms to keep from dragging his smug brother across the desk and planting him a well-deserved facer. Yes, Gabriel had become far better at this baiting business than he'd have ever credited. "And just what will I have to do to—?"

"A chaperone."

Alex angled his head, giving a look about for this mysteriously appearing chaperone.

"You are to act as chaperone for Chloe."

A laugh exploded from his chest. "Surely you j-jest." He shook with the force of his amusement. His brother still had traces of the humor he'd once possessed. Well, this was a good deal more reassuring than the unpleasant alternative that he'd become, God forbid . . . their father. Alex yanked a crisp kerchief from the front of his jacket and dabbed at the tears of mirth in his eyes, then looked at Gabriel.

His brother fixed a black glower on him. Well, rot. He'd not been jesting. Alex stuffed away his kerchief, amusement fading.

His brother continued. "Chloe requires chaperoning."

He groaned. Gabriel would task him with squiring his sister about to dull, polite, and proper *ton* events?

Gabriel continued his reasoning. "With Mother in the country with Philippa during her confinement, Chloe needs to be escorted about the *ton*."

A shudder wracked Alex's frame. He'd made it a point to avoid those boring pastimes for nearly ten years now. Perhaps he'd try reasoning with Gabriel. After all, the other man had always been the practical . . . well, reasonable one. "Surely you recognize the folly in *me*," he splayed his hands, "chaperoning our youngest sister. You are by far the better man for the ta . . ." His brother narrowed his eyes even more. Christ. "Er . . . for the taking her about town bit," he cleverly substituted.

Gabriel drummed his fingers on his seat. "I have taken her about town." He held a finger up. "More precisely, I've taken Chloe *and* Philippa about. It is because of me that Philippa has been properly wed." To Lord Winston, a stodgy bore who didn't smile enough in Alex's estimation. "You should consider yourself fortunate you've just the one to chaperone."

He'd wager the lifetime's worth of his allowance that not a single peer in the realm would affix the title "chaperone" to his given name.

"Since there is nothing of value you contribute to the family," his brother spoke in effortless disparagement, "this is something you can do." That handful of words was more than just a little condescending in the aspersions they cast upon his character.

Filled with restiveness, Alex shoved to his feet. "Bah, this isn't about proving my worth." He made for the other man's sideboard in desperate need of liquid fortitude. He swiped the nearest bottle and a glass, then poured himself a stiff brandy. "This is about you shifting your responsibilities." He held the glass up in salute and then took a long swallow.

Gabriel's gaze grew shuttered once more and Alex knew, with that slight raising of his glass and the impulsive words he'd tossed at his brother's smug face, he'd gone and shattered any hope of being relieved of this task. "If you can manage to find some scrap of decency in you, you'll know I have never shifted responsibilities."

"Unlike me?"

His brother lounged in his chair, as though bored by the whole discourse. "You refused a position in the clergy," he pointed out.

He, Lord Alex Edgerton of the cloth? Alex gave his head a rueful shake. The devil would have danced in delight with the hilarity of it.

Taking Alex's silence for an invitation to continue presenting his case, Gabriel added, "Nor were you interested in a commission in the King's army."

Alex swirled the contents of his glass, stoically silent. He quite enjoyed life and hadn't relished the prospect of marching to the beat of a drum, potentially risking life and limb . . . and his visual appeal. After all, that was really all he had to contribute to Society. Not much of a contribution, but there you had it. Boney's eventual takeover of the Continent had proven his remarkable foresight.

An exasperated sigh escaped his brother, proving silence to be the most effective strategy in handling Gabriel when he was on one of his lectures. "You may resume your shiftless life, drinking yourself into oblivion and whoremongering . . ."

Alex enjoyed the pleasures to be found in a woman's arms "Whoremongerer, am I?" he said with droll humor in his tone. Other than the eager widows, he didn't dally with respectable ladies. Long ago he'd learned societal ladies in the market for a husband had little use for a second son. No, he would not open himself up to hurt in giving any more of himself; not when life had taught him the perils in hoping for love—from anyone.

"When Chloe is wed," his brother went on. "When she is married, then you'll be free to live your purposeless life." He gave a flick of his hand and dragged forth a ledger. With precise, methodical movements, the other man flipped it open, picked up his pen, and proceeded to work.

A seething rage thrummed through Alex as he stared at the bent head, black hair so similar to his own that many had often said the two men could be mirrors of one another. Their bond had once been that close, forged by years of their father's abuse. How easily Gabriel had forgotten. Everything. Every lash. Every thwack of the birch wood as it was applied to their buttocks. An old familiar fury and pain roiled in his gut. May his father's dark soul burn in hell for his sins. Alex would never forgive his long-departed sire. But Gabriel's crimes were far greater. For Alex and Gabriel had been more than friends—they'd been brothers, and yet how easily the other man had forgotten all they'd suffered through.

Alex downed the contents of his glass in a long, slow swallow and grimaced at the fiery trail it blazed. Knowing it would infuriate the stiffly proper marquess, he swiped the half-empty decanter from the Chippendale sideboard and started for the door, needing to be free of the other man's sight. He shot a glance over his shoulder. "Oh, Gabriel?"

His brother paused, pen poised over the ledger, and glanced up with a question in his eyes.

Alex inclined his head. "Congratulations. You would make Father proud with the man you've become."

Those words had the intended effect. Gabriel recoiled and sat unblinking; the lines of his face a hard, unmovable mask.

Yet, that small victory left Alex hollow as he took his leave. "Chaperone." He suppressed a groan. Then, it could be a good deal worse. Alex stomped his way down the red-carpeted corridors, his boots noiseless in the wide halls. At least he enjoyed Chloe's company. If he were being totally truthful, with her tendency to seek out and find trouble, she was the most entertaining of his siblings. Philippa had always been the proper, polite one. No wonder she'd wed a stodgy bore handpicked by their brother.

Alex reached the end of the hall and continued onward to the library. As much as he abhorred this room for the memories here, it had become a sanctuary of sorts. Largely because not a single servant or sibling would dare look for him there. That understanding had proven quite beneficial through the years. He pressed the handle and slipped inside, closing the door behind him.

"Chaperone," he muttered. "Sooner lob off my arm than act as a chaperone." And Gabriel knew that and it was likely why he'd given him the honor. Alex claimed a seat on one of the leather sofas and set down the brandy and glass. He splashed several fingers into the crystal snifter, and then thought better of it. "Chaperone." With a wry shake of his head, he filled the glass to the brim.

The floorboard creaked and he stiffened. He passed his gaze about the empty room and then returned his attention to the task doled out by his bastard of a brother. How difficult could it be to wed Chloe off? To a man who was not a stodgy bore, as Gabriel would have seen her wedded to? With her spirit, she at least deserved a fun chap. Alex frowned into the contents of his glass. Not one of the rakish sorts who visited the notorious hells that Alex himself frequented. Perhaps a stodgy bore might be better for her, after all.

He nursed the amber contents of his drink. With each sip, the hot fury burning his chest eased. He'd always known his father had despised him and Alex had scars enough for proof. Gabriel, on the other hand, hadn't always been filled with this antipathy for him. No, at one time, he and Gabriel had shared such a bond. Alex would have gladly given his life for Gabriel. Back when he'd been hopelessly naïve, he'd thought those sentiments returned. Everything had changed the day their cold bastard of a sire had noted his heir was no longer a child and had taken him under his heartless wing, instilling in him all those necessary lessons for a future marquess.

From then on, Alex had ceased to exist. To both of them. He swirled the contents of his glass. Which was, in a way, a favor done him, if an unwitting one, by Gabriel. For then, the beatings had stopped. He tightened his hands reflexively about the glass. His one regret had been that his evil sire had not known the man he'd become because by God, laws of nature be damned, he'd have gladly traded blow for blow with the other man.

Seated in the quiet of his brother's library, he recognized there were certainly things a good deal worse than chaperoning Chloe for the remainder of the Season. His father had taught him that.

Chapter 3

*T*he next day, after Chloe had concocted her desperate scheme to reintroduce Imogen into polite Society, Imogen found herself with her back pressed against the Marquess of Waverly's leather sofa. With her friend's head bent over one scandal sheet or another, Imogen appreciated just how far she herself had fallen.

Imogen sighed. Three days, just thirty-six hours away from being a duchess in love with her husband, and not even five months later—*this*. Copies of papers lay spread out before them in messy piles and two dull pencils rested atop them. Imogen gave her head a pathetic shake. As though any strategy could silence the gossips. Wherever the *ton* was, so too would be the story of her and the Duke of Montrose and the sister he really loved.

The D of M forsakes all for love.

Had a lesser lord, or any other gentleman for that matter, thrown Imogen over for her sister, the cad would have been held in the ranks of Boney himself. But it was a duke and somehow Society had made his betrayal into something romantic. She'd never understand the *ton*. Nor did she *care* to understand a people so callous as to delight in another person's woes.

Imogen shifted her shoulders, her lower back aching from the stiff position they'd been in since Lord Alex had invaded the library. "Can't we simply announce ourselves?" she mouthed.

Chloe frowned her into silence and gave her head a brusque shake.

She reached for the morning copy of *The Times*. Her friend flicked her hand and she winced. "What was that—?"

"Hush," she whispered, pressing a finger to her lips.

Imogen settled back in her seat. By the clink of glass touching glass, Lord Alex Edgerton intended to stay, and would probably get himself soused. In a library. By himself. Which likely meant she was stuck here for as long as her friend decided they were to be . . . well, stuck here. Or, until the gentleman drank himself into oblivion. Imogen had little experience on the matters of overindulging gentleman and their intoxicated states. "This is silly," she mouthed. Though in truth, she'd spent too many days since William's betrayal being a sad, somber lady she no longer recognized. A renewed thrill surged through her as she embraced the lighthearted woman she'd once been—even if but for a moment.

Chloe slapped a finger to her lips. "Sometimes he speaks to himself." She leaned closer and whispered in her ear. "I've gathered some rather useful pieces of information."

The "he" in question was none other than Chloe's brother. Not the respectable Marquess of Waverly, but rather, the other brother who'd moments ago mumbled something about lobbing his chaperone's arm off. Though why he had a chaperone, she'd be hard pressed to guess. He was also one who likely broke hearts and if he had betrothed himself to a lady, broke that very important tie and . . .

A growl escaped her.

Chloe slammed an elbow into her side once more.

"Ouch—"

"Hullo, ladies."

They shrieked and, in unison, jerked their heads up. Lord Alex leaned over the edge of the sofa. Imogen stared at the upside down, grinning visage of the notoriously rakish *gentleman*. With a day's growth of beard on the harsh, angular planes of his cheeks, he peered down at her through bloodshot green eyes, likely from too much drink and carousing. She really wished she'd not noticed what a splendid specimen of a figure he was, for she'd already learned the perils of those rakish, handsome sorts. As though noting her perusal, Lord Alex winked. Heat slapped her cheeks and Imogen jerked her head forward.

"Alex!" Chloe exclaimed, jumping up. With far greater reluctance, Imogen came to her feet beside her. "Whatever are you doing here?" For her flare for the dramatics all these years, she was a dreadful actress. "I had no idea you were here."

Lord Alex unfolded to his full, towering height, glass of spirits in hand. "By here, do you mean in this library where you were before I made my entrance?"

His sister swatted him on the arm. "You're unpardonable."

A half grin turned his firm lips up. An odd, fluttery sensation danced in Imogen's chest and she was grateful when brother and sister launched into a familial discussion on who was the more bothersome Edgerton sibling. She used the distraction as a moment to study him; this rogue sought after by all manner of scandalous ladies. Where her former betrothed had been lean and possessed of a golden perfection, Lord Alex Edgerton could not be more different than the duke who'd broken her heart. More than a foot taller than her own five foot three inches, Lord Alex's muscle-hewn frame had the power to command a room. Whispered about by all the ladies, innocent and otherwise, there was nothing proper or respectable about the bachelor. With his seductive winks and sly grins, he represented folly. As though feeling her gaze upon him, Lord Alex slid his stare in her direction, assessing her through thick lashes. Imogen's heart quickened. *Folly, indeed.* She gave silent thanks when Chloe said something calling his attention back.

Just then, he tossed his head back and bellowed with laughter. The subtle movement sent a strand of black hair falling over his brow. She angled her head and took in the gentleness of his eyes as he conversed. This man she'd only known to be a rogue proved himself to be something more—a teasing brother. She'd learned to protect herself against the rakish types. This loyal, devoted stranger was an altogether different matter. With his regard for Chloe, Lord Alex chipped away at some of the cynical, preconceived notions she'd carried of him these past years.

Imogen forcibly thrust back the thoughts that might soften her to the notorious rake. Instead, she fixed on that midnight lock over his eye. *Dark like sin,* a voice whispered. A sad smile turned her lips at the corner. Then, a gentleman more golden than the legendary Apollo had betrayed her. She waited for the familiar twinge of pain. But it did not come.

Lord Alex looked to her once more and issued a belated greeting. "Lady Gwendolyn," he bowed. "A pleasure as always."

"Imogen," she squeezed out through gritted teeth. Was she invisible to everyone?

"If you insist on such informality then, Imogen," he said with another one of those wicked winks.

She opened her mouth and closed it several times. The scoundrel had merely tricked her into giving him leave to use her Christian name. A bounder, indeed. Why did her heart kick up a beat?

Lord Alexander reclaimed his seat and reached for a partially empty bottle of brandy. He tipped it and proceeded to fill his empty glass.

Imogen widened her eyes. Why . . . why . . . He intended to sit and indulge in spirits. Here. Now? *And* refer to her by her Christian name? "But . . ."

He paused midpour and gave her a questioning look. "Yes, Imogen?"

By the teasing glint in his eyes, she knew he expected her to scold him for his high-handedness. Imogen gave her head a slight shake, tired of being the boring, predictable lady. "Nothing at all," she bit out, resenting it perhaps as much as she detested the pitying glances she garnered from everyone except her still gleeful mother. Oh, how disappointed her late Papa would have been of his wife's mercenary grasping for that coveted title. Loyal to a fault, he would have been almost as disappointed in his wife as with Rosalind's behavior; gloating over the title duchess she'd snared, uncaring that her elder sister's heart had been breaking. *That* was the true pain that remained of the hasty marriage between the Duke and Duchess of Montrose.

"Dare I ask what has you ladies hiding away in the library?" Lord Alex asked, giving his glass a slow swirl.

"Nothing," Imogen said quickly. It brought his head up. Too quickly. She trained her gaze on Chloe. They'd been friends so long they often gleaned one another's unspoken thoughts.

Chloe stooped to rescue their collection of scandal sheets. "Oh, we're merely pouring through the gossip columns," she said. Apparently, her friend didn't know her quite as well as she'd hoped. Imogen gave her a silencing look. "We're trying to ascertain the least popular events to attend." A silencing look her friend studiously ignored.

"Indeed," he drawled. Fortunately, Lord Alex sounded about as interested as if his sister had announced their intentions to take their vows in the church and have him serve as witness.

"Oh, yes."

Imogen fought back a groan. *Please stop talking.*

"We're taking care to avoid the crushes." Chloe waved a hand about. "Those events where all the most popular gossips are in attendance. You see, that has been my clever plan to—" Imogen stepped on her toes. "Did you just step on my toes?" Chloe asked it with the same shock as if Imogen had turned her puppy into cherry tarts.

"My foot slipped," she muttered, with that slight, but none-too-subtle gesture.

Lord Alex attended them with real interest, now.

Splendid.

Her friend gave her a long, commiserative look, which bordered too close to that pitying kind. She glanced away.

"Well?" Lord Alex prodded. "Out with it."

Chloe firmed her lips and shook her head once. *Now she would be silent?* Well, there was something for at least belated awareness.

In one effortless move, Alex leaned across the sofa and plucked the copy of *The Times* from his sister. Imogen's breath caught as his well-muscled forearm brushed her shoulder. "Thank you," he said under his breath. He proceeded to skim the front page.

Embarrassment drove back the momentary lapse in sanity his innocuous touch had roused as he skimmed the pages of the scandal sheet that documented her shame. Imogen shifted back and forth on her feet, making a show of studying the room. Her gaze collided with Chloe's.

Sorry, her friend mouthed, and then turned with a flounce to her brother. "It isn't really well-done, reading the scandal pages," she said the way a nursemaid might deliver a setdown.

"No, it isn't," he murmured, not taking his eyes off the page. "You really should refrain from that." Then Lord Alex looked up from the page. He met Imogen's gaze square on. She tipped her chin up a notch. Daring him to say a blasted thing of the dastardly duke and her duplicitous sister. All of it. Any of it.

"Here," he tossed the paper over to his sister who effortlessly caught it. "All rubbish, that."

Imogen swallowed hard. Lord Alex was correct. At his unspoken defense, warmth slipped into her heart and, for the first time in a long time, she acknowledged the truth of that. It was all rubbish. Every last bit of it. After months of dwelling on the hurtful gossip, there was something freeing in that sudden realization.

"That is all you'll say?" her friend exclaimed, cutting into this momentary weakening of the shockingly gallant gentleman.

"Chloe," she began. She appreciated her friend's loyalty, but she also craved her discretion. Even if the bounder before them was only her brother, the indolent Lord Alex.

"Oh, uh, yes. Well, then." Chloe gave a flounce of her curls, this time correctly interpreting Imogen's silent pleading.

"What would you have me say?"

Nothing. She'd have him say nothing about the scandal, or her broken betrothal, and assuredly nothing about His Grace, the Duke of Montrose.

Both ladies exchanged a look.

He took another swallow of his brandy. "I suppose I could say any lady would be fortunate to avoid marriage to the arrogant fop." With that, he tossed back the remaining contents.

That. I would have you say that. Chloe laughed and spared Imogen from finding words. Her heart quickened. He could say that particular something about her humiliation. Lord Alex returned his gaze to her, a dark glint in his cynical eyes. Then the warm, fluttery sensation in her chest was extinguished with a reminder of the truth—with his glib tongue and right words, he was no different than any other rogue. It would be silly to serve as voyeur to this exchange between Lord Alex and Chloe and form any opinion but the one she'd gleaned of him over the years.

"I daresay I'd rather wed a mere second son than a lofty duke who'd break a lady's heart," Chloe said, in a bid to be supportive.

Imogen's cheeks flooded with heat.

Lord Alex gave a mock shudder. "Egad, that will be a dark day, indeed, when young ladies decide to turn their attentions upon the lesser second sons." He winked. "After all, avoiding the parson's trap is the sole benefit of being that lesser, second son." Even with the crooked grin, the hard twist of his lips spoke of a cynical rogue who avoided any hint of respectable misses.

"Oh, hush, Alex. Why, someday you shall fall in love and I will quite gleefully remind you of what a foul fiend you were," his sister said, giving him a slight shove. "Isn't that right, Imogen?"

A rake with his chiseled cheeks and noble jaw likely had any number of women falling in love with him on any given day. She shifted. "Your brother has the right of it," she said softly. Another tug pulled at Imogen's heart; a wish for more.

He trained his stare on her once again, in that bold, assessing way.

Did he expect she'd look away? She met his gaze squarely. She'd been the subservient, deferential young lady once before. Never again. Imogen angled her chin up.

Alex refilled his snifter and made to take a sip of his brandy, then froze, the glass midway to his lips. Imogen met his gaze with a boldness he'd not expected of a miss of nineteen, twenty years? The blues of her eyes may as well have been a mirror to his own dark cynicism on the sentiments of love and yet he glimpsed past that, to the emotion in the sapphire depths. He didn't make it a habit of noticing anything where a young, unwed lady was concerned. With a silent curse, he tossed back a long swallow, grimacing at the trail it blazed down his throat. The chit had the widest eyes and the most generous mouth, full lips made for sin, and . . .

He choked on his brandy. For the love of God, what madness possessed him that he'd do something as insensible as lusting after Lady Imogen Moore?

"Oh, dear," Chloe exclaimed, a suspicious glint in her eyes. "Are you all right?"

"Fine," he gritted out. With her temerity in all matters over the years, he knew she'd not be content with that succinct utterance.

She leaned forward and squinted. "I do say, your face is all flushed. Do you notice, Imogen?" Chloe poked him in the cheek and he swatted her hand away.

Imogen's lips twitched and the lady's unfiltered amusement softened her face. All thought fled as he was sucked in by the smile on her full lips. She tipped her head and made a show of studying him. Only, if she *truly* studied him, she'd see the havoc she now wrought on his senses. "I daresay your brother will be just fine," she assured his sister, not appearing the slightest bit concerned with whether he did, in fact, end up just fine.

And here he'd been mooning over her and—he shuddered—her innocent smile? Madness, indeed. He bristled, unaccustomed to being so dismissed by a lady. Why, ladies young and old clamored for his notice, for reasons that had nothing to do with a title and everything to do with the reputation he'd earned behind chamber doors. With a frown, he finished the remainder of his drink, deliberately ignoring the two vexing misses.

Except Imogen touched a finger against the tip of her lower lip, drawing his attention once more to the lush mouth . . .

And he choked on his swallow.

She creased her brow. "Oh, dear perhaps there is, in fact, something wrong." Though the light twinkle in her eyes indicated the lady was having a good deal of fun at his expense.

Which young ladies assuredly did not do. They had fun with him, in ways that would make this teasing vixen's cheeks burn with shocked outrage and certainly not in any way that was respectable.

"I assure you, I'm indeed fine," he drawled. Alex set his glass down. He really should leave. Instead, he wandered around to the back of the sofa. He glanced down at the piles of scandal sheets scattered about the floor and toed the copies. They really had amassed quite the collection. "I daresay I'd expect you'd be so thorough as to have *The* Ton's *Tattler* in your pile," he said dryly.

Chloe gasped. "How could I have failed to procure a copy?" She sprinted toward the door.

"Where are you going?" he called after her.

"To have one of the footman secure a copy," she shot back without breaking her stride.

He gave his head a rueful shake and looked down once more. His lips twitched and when he picked his head up, Imogen's cheeks were red like a summer berry. Which only roused delicious images of the young lady upon satin sheets while he dipped berries in champagne and . . . With a silent curse he kicked at the untidy stack. "Quite a bit of reading you ladies are doing."

She smiled. "Your sister's idea."

Once more he admired Imogen's generous smile, noting the faintest dimple in her right cheek, which transformed her from something ordinary into someone really quite . . . *extraordinary*. "If it is my sister's idea, it is assuredly a bad one," he said at last and wandered over to fetch his bottle of brandy and empty glass. Imogen stared and smiled with a woman's cheek and yet blushed like a young girl just from the schoolroom.

If he was noticing Lady Imogen's smile, he needed a drink. He filled his glass.

"Do you make it a habit of drinking at this early hour?"

He'd have to be deaf to fail to hear the trace of disapproval in that question. "Yes." He took a long sip.

She pursed her lips. "Do you also make it a habit of drinking spirits in front of unwed young ladies?"

God, the termagant was tenacious. He preferred her smiling. "No," he said solemnly. He gave her a slow, seductive grin. "I make it a habit of avoiding unwed young ladies altogether."

She muttered something under her breath.

He would have wagered the allowance his brother now threatened him with that she'd said something about "those fortunate young ladies." And standing there alone with Lady Tart-Mouth, it occurred to him the lady did not like him. Hmm. This was interesting, indeed. Of course, preferable, as he didn't need innocents seeking his favor, but still interesting.

Alex propped his hip on the arm of the sofa. "You don't like me much, do you, Imogen?"

"I don't know you, Lord Alex." He gave her a look. After all, she and Chloe had been inseparable through the years. "That is, I don't *really* know you," she added quickly. Too quickly. Imogen cast a hopeful-looking glance toward the door, likely praying for his sister's swift return.

He, on the other hand, wished Chloe all manner of delays in her quest for the scandal sheet he'd sent her in search of. "Come, Imogen we've known each other some years now." The young lady had gone to finishing school with his youngest sister. He'd made a studious point of avoiding the giggling, chatting young ladies over the years. Beyond Imogen's scandal with Montrose, he knew nothing more about her.

"No." She shook her head wildly, dislodging a burnt-red tress. "I've known your sister for years. You, I know not at all." Nor did she sound at all enthused about furthering an acquaintance. The stern rebuke underlining her words only roused his dawning interest in the lovely Lady Imogen with her sunset curls piled atop her head.

Alex shoved himself from a position of repose and wandered close. "We are, in the very least, family friends." He stopped a hairsbreadth from her, until Imogen was forced to retreat or glance up. "Enough that you should call me by my Christian name," he whispered, unknowing why he should find such interest in the disapproving minx.

She took several hasty steps backward and ran her palms over the front of her skirts. "I would not . . . it would not be appropriate." The word appropriate had no place on a mouth such as hers.

The telltale tremble to her long fingers drew his attention and spoke to her awareness of him. Awareness from the bold widows he took his pleasure with was welcome. Awareness from the flush-faced, white-skirt-wearing innocents was dangerous.

He set his glass down on the table and continued his advance. "It would only be appropriate considering you've given me leave to use your Christian name, Imogen."

This time she remained rooted to the floor. She tossed her chin up. The movement dislodged another orange-red tress. "I did not give you leave to use my Christian name. You stole the use of it by tricking me."

He caught the two strands and tucked one behind her ear. "Yes, yes I did." The other silken lock he rubbed between his thumb and forefinger. If one could capture a sunset, this would be the feel. Hot and silken. Alex blinked several times and released her quickly. He stumbled over himself in his haste to be away from her.

"Is everything all right, Lord Alexander?" Concern filled her eyes, once more affirming the staggering, if humbling, truth. The chit was a good deal less aware of him than he'd believed.

"Alex," he corrected.

Imogen hesitated. "Alex," she said at last, the one-syllable utterance, his name seeming to be dragged from her. Still, for the caution there, her low, husky tone wrapped about him.

He jerked his chin toward the stacks of scandal sheets containing the lady's name. "And what of this plan my sister spoke of? I gather it pertains to Montrose." She really was no different than any other English lady captivated by a duke, longing for that coveted title.

Imogen blushed, dropping her gaze to the pages behind the sofa. "It's really not polite of you to speak of—" She clamped her lips tight, leaving the thought unfinished.

And then it occurred to him . . . "Never tell me you fancied yourself in love with the man," he scoffed.

The lady met his gaze. A glimmer of pity shone from the depths of her blue eyes. "I'd not expect one of your reputation to understand."

Annoyance stabbed at him. No man preferred to be the object of pity, particularly not where a fiery-haired beauty such as Lady Imogen Moore was concerned. "I understand a good deal more than you believe."

"You do?" She fluttered a hand about her chest, momentarily bringing his attention to the generous swell of her décolletage. How had he not ever before appreciated those full breasts?

"Undoubtedly," he managed to dredge up a response. "What lady doesn't aspire to the title duchess?" Or really, *any* titled lord, but never that second son.

"Is that what you believe?" her question, a barely there whisper, floated to him.

"Is there any other reason to desire a conceited fop like Montrose for one's husband?" The glittering world of their Society had proven women faithless, fickle creatures who'd make the most advantageous match and then take their pleasures where they saw fit. Usually in his bed.

Fire lit her eyes and threatened to set him ablaze with the intensity of her stare. "That is hardly proper discourse for a lady and a gentleman, and one who is practically a stranger."

"A family friend," he reminded her. "And if you are this polite, it is no wonder that he—"

Imogen shot a hand out and cracked him on the cheek with her palm.

The force of her blow sent his head reeling to the side. He flexed his jaw. Well, the lady could deliver quite a blow, and if he were being truthful with himself, it was a well-deserved one.

Horror filled her face. "I . . . Oh my . . . I . . . ." Usually such stammering and incoherence was reserved for behind chamber doors. Though he suspected he'd have more of a likelihood of rousing such sentiments in any one of the most staid matrons at Almack's than this disapproving young lady.

He waved a hand. "No apologies are necessary, my lady." Imogen, with her proud indignation, rose in his estimation. "That was uncalled for on my part." He'd not debate the veracity of his words with her on the merits of ladies of the *ton* who carefully guarded their reputations and, when they eventually married, sought out the spare to an heir.

"It was," Imogen said unapologetically. "Rude of you, that is." She clasped her hands together and studied the interlocked digits. "Still, it would not do to hit you, Lord . . . Alex," she amended at his pointed look.

"I have it!"

Their gazes swung in unison to the door. Chloe brandished a copy of the scandal page, a triumphant glimmer in her eyes. Then her smile died. She looked back and forth between him and Imogen. "What is it?"

Alex sketched a low bow. "Imogen was merely saying how anxious she was to begin your plan." Whatever cracked scheme his sister had concocted.

Imogen's eyebrows shot up.

"Splendid," Chloe said with a widening smile.

Alex winked at Imogen and took his leave. At last, he knew what could be a good deal worse than being tasked with the role of chaperone.

It would be serving as a chaperone to that tart-mouthed, fiery crimson-curled young lady.

Chapter 4

The following afternoon, in the marble foyer of his brother's home, Alex pulled out his watch fob and consulted the gold timepiece. She was late. Nearly thirty-minutes late, and he noted that particular detail not because he gave a jot about timeliness or any such nonsense, but rather, until he saw to his responsibility, then he was otherwise prevented from spending his day as he wished—at his faro tables with a delectable beauty his only desired company for the night.

With a silent curse, he glanced up the staircase for a hint of his sister, damning Gabriel to the devil for the thousandth time that day. Chaperone. On a trip to Bond Street. Alex shuddered. The devil was likely exacting his due for all the sinful deeds Alex had been guilty of through the years. Bedding widows and other light-skirts. The excessive wagering. Oh, he had little plan to cease his roguish ways, but he could appreciate that his brother sought to punish the badness out of him.

Hadn't Gabriel realized their father had tried at that? Tried and failed. Alex gave his head a disgusted shake. He should be at Forbidden Pleasures, a crimson beauty with a lush mouth and blue eyes curled on his lap. The rapid flow of thoughts came to a jarring halt. "Where in hell did that come from?"

"Where did what come from, sir?" the old, gray-haired butler asked in nasal tones.

He spun about. "Bloody hell, Joseph, must you scare a man?"

The ghost of a smile played about the lips of the servant who'd been with their family since the old monster of a marquess had been alive and in power, beating his children and . . . "My apologies, sir." He held out Alex's cloak.

With a murmured "thanks," Alex shrugged into it. He shot another look up the staircase just as his sister appeared. "I'm so very glad you are able to join me."

Joseph grinned, coughing into his hand to hide the expression of amusement.

Either ignoring or failing to hear his droll words, his sister bounded down the steps with a lack of ladylike decorum that would have shocked their mother. Alex had ceased being shocked by anyone and anything when he'd been a child who'd felt the fury of his father's fists.

"Alex," she greeted with a smile as a footman rushed over with her cloak. "I hope you were not waiting long."

"I was." For a shopping trip that he wanted nothing to do with. The only shops he visited were to select fine baubles for well-sated mistresses, not wherever it is unwed innocents like his sister visited.

Joseph pulled the door open.

As though she'd not heard the dry reproach in his words, Chloe sailed outside and made her way to the waiting carriage. "I'm quite looking forward to our trip shopping."

"You've never enjoyed a trip to Bond Street," he mumbled. Not as a small girl when he'd thought to do a brotherly good deed and take her to the Bond Street Bazaar and not when she'd been a lady who'd made her Come Out and he'd escorted her one last time for a bonnet. Or had it been a ribbon?

Chloe beamed and tugged on her gloves. "No, that is true." With that odd statement, she continued on, prattling about their plans for the afternoon, and then the evening, and then tomorrow evening and . . . God help him. They reached the front of the carriage and she gave a set of directions to the driver. She resumed her blurred ramblings. "First we shall collect Imogen and . . ."

He blinked. "What?" Alex shot a hand out and blocked his sister's ascent into the black-lacquered conveyance.

"We're to visit Bond Street." Her lips formed a small moue of displeasure. "Do you listen to nothing I say?" She slipped under his arm and scrambled into the carriage sans assistance.

With a silent curse, he climbed in after her. "Not that particular detail, Chloe. The other part." About the tart-mouthed, crimson-curled beauty.

Chloe wrinkled her brow. "Do you refer to Imogen? Yes. We are to collect her." A beleaguered sigh she'd likely learned at their mama's knee, escaped her. "Really, Alex, I swear you listen to nothing I say."

"I'm fairly certain you'd not mentioned this particular detail," he said impatiently. This, this he would remember. Particularly after their volatile exchange yesterday morning.

"I didn't?"

"You did not."

A footman closed the door behind them and then the driver snapped the reins. The carriage lurched forward.

Chloe lifted her shoulders in a nonchalant shrug. "Regardless, even you realize we simply cannot leave her to her family. That wouldn't be at all something a friend would do."

That is hardly proper discourse for a lady and a gentleman, and one who is practically a stranger. Considering the lady's words and the fact that his skin still stung from her slap, there were no feelings of friendship on either of their parts. "No." He'd been charged with chaperoning his sister. He'd not be tasked with the Lady Imogen and her disapproving eyes or frowning lips.

They are not always frowning. Sometimes they turn up in a seductive, enticing pull . . .

Chloe folded her arms mutinously across her chest. "Yes."

He opened his mouth to call orders for the carriage to continue on directly to Bond Street, but an uncharacteristic somberness in his sister's eyes stifled the words.

"Please, Alex. She cannot be alone. She is quite looking forward to this outing." Of course. The trip to the shops at the famed shopping district had nothing to do with his pragmatic sister and everything to do with the young woman who'd snared and then lost a duke. "Surely you see she requires all the support she can find. It really is all rather tragic." His sister's lower lip trembled, hinting at the sadness she carried.

He shifted on the bench and resisted the urge to direct his eyes to the ceiling. "Tragic?"

"Her heart has been broken, Alex. She loved him."

He snorted. "She loved his title."

Chloe recoiled as though slapped. "How can you say that?"

"Rather easily," he said with a bluntness that made her flinch. Guilt stirred, but he shoved it back. His sister's naïveté and innocence would be the ruin of her if he weren't careful. Perhaps he was the better chaperone for her, after all. His stodgy, stiff brother would fail to see the perils abounding throughout London for one such as Chloe.

"You are wrong, Alexander Nicholas Edgerton. She loved him and—"

"I thought you didn't believe in love." That jaded piece of his sister, another product of their father's cruel influence.

She blinked "I don't for myself, I do for others, and most especially for my dear friend. Surely that makes sense."

Something twisted inside him. Other young ladies her age were to have starry hopes of love and happily-ever-afters and all other drivel Alex himself didn't believe in. But damn it, he wanted it for his sister and loathed his dead father all the more for having robbed Chloe of her innocence. She leaned over and flicked his hand. "Do not change the subject, Alex. She loved him and it had nothing to do with his title."

He snorted.

Chloe's frown deepened. "Whenever did you become so cynical?"

"Too long ago to remember," he said with a smile for his sister.

She pointed her eyes to the ceiling of the carriage then shifted her attention to the window, studiously ignoring him.

With her disapproval came blessed silence. The carriage continued to rattle along the cobbled London streets. Alex settled back in the comfortable, red velvet squabs. His sister believed he'd given her a sarcastic nonanswer. Except his had been, mayhap, one of the most truthful pieces he'd imparted. The birth of his cynicism, as Chloe had called it, came somewhere between a birch rod upon his back as a child of seven and the day he'd left university. It had taken but his first ball to discover there was a whole host of *ladies* with a preference for the spare to the heir who brought no marriage-worthy connection.

The carriage rocked to a halt before a white, stucco townhouse. He yanked back the curtain. "Bloody wonderful," he groaned. "Oomph. Will you please stop kicking me," he bit out.

"Only if you cease being so foul."

For all that was holy, this chaperone business was not worth his allowance. It was not. "What was that for?"

She fixed a glower on him. "Be nice."

"I'm always nice," he groused.

"No, you're not." Chloe jabbed her finger out. "You're only charming to the scandalous ladies with their dampened gowns." He choked. What did his sister know of scandalous ladies and dampened gowns? No, he really didn't care to know. Chloe went on. "You're improper and you wear a horribly scandalous grin. I'll not have you be that way around Imogen."

Well, then. Alex sat back, silenced by his younger sister. Of all the humbling . . .

"And furthermore—"

That furthermore went blessedly unfinished as the driver pulled open the carriage door.

Imogen accepted the servant's hand and then their gazes locked. Something volatile and charged passed between them and, for an infinitesimal moment, everything slipped away, but for her. Her fathomless blue eyes formed wide circles and she remained there, one foot poised on the floor of the carriage, the other hanging out. "You." Shock underscored that one word utterance.

Had she expected Prinny himself? This lady who'd drag his sister along on a shopping trip? He folded his arms. "Tell me, my lady, do you intend to stand frozen like a Greek stone statue all afternoon or do you intend to join my sister on *her* shopping trip?" He winced as his sister kicked him again.

"I said be nice," she hissed. Chloe shouldered him out of the way and motioned Imogen inside the Marquess of

Waverly's extravagant, spacious landau. "Do forgive him," Chloe said, her tone apologetic. "He is quite foul, you know."

"Indeed," the lady muttered under her breath.

Alex bristled and made room on the bench for Lady Tart-Mouth.

Imogen hesitated and then claimed the seat on the bench alongside Chloe. Which, of course, made total, perfect, proper sense. And also filled him with an inexplicable disappointment.

Imogen quickly worked her gaze over the carriage. "Where is your brother?" she blurted.

"I am her brother," he snapped before his sister could formulate a proper reply.

"I referred to her *eldest* brother."

As in Gabriel, the favored Marquess of Waverly. It mattered not of the man's character or principle, only the size of his pockets and the age of his title. His lip peeled back in a sneer. "Do you refer to the marquess?"

"Is there another?" She scratched her brow.

"There is not." It would not have surprised Alex to discover his reprehensible father had sired a passel of brats on some outrageous woman or another. *With your profligate ways, are you really very different?* A needling voice taunted. Even though he'd taken care to not get his child upon a woman, he conducted himself in much the same way. The ugly, unpleasant truth fueled his ire. "And you'd, of course, prefer Waverly because of that marquess title." He ignored Chloe's sharp gasp.

"I'd prefer the marquess because he's respectable." Imogen gave him a pointed look. "And he is *not* a rogue."

At her insolent tone, he narrowed his eyes. "*And* you are disappointed there is no marquess to work your charms upon."

Imogen snorted. "If I possessed any charms worth mentioning, I'd have used them upon my own betrothed." Her droll words cut into his anger, drove it back, and in the dark confines of the carriage, he peered at her. That had certainly not been the outraged reaction he'd sought to elicit from the lady.

Mouth agape, Chloe alternated her stare between them.

Alex set his jaw and settled back in his seat, not for the first time cursing Gabriel and his damned plans for Alex and his independence.

The scandal sheets had reported with some frequency on Lord Alex Edgerton. In all of those pieces she'd read with only barely there interest, they'd labeled him a charming, affable, if cynical, rogue.

Imogen found the gentleman to be a good deal less than affable.

In the stilted quiet of the carriage, she studied him. With his unfashionably long, black hair and dark-green, nearly black eyes, there was something dark and menacing about him. The papers also purported he was known to carry on with anyone from a scandalous widow to an unhappily wedded lady. And so for the dark, hard beauty of him, she'd never see anything more than a shameless cad who belonged with the ranks of the Montroses of the world. Why, she didn't feel so much as the faintest stirring of interest in the gentleman. He may as well have been—Alex shifted his gaze to her, piercing her with the intensity of his stare.

Her heart sped up. *Liar.* She jerked her attention to the window. She'd noticed him. A good deal more than she should. A good deal more than was safe. *Was any manner of interest in Lord Alex Edgerton safe?*

The carriage rocked to a sudden halt. "We're here," Chloe said with a wide smile.

Relief warred with unease as Imogen faced the prospect of stepping out into Society once more, this time as the jilted bride, thrown over for her sister. The driver pulled the door open and helped Chloe out. Alex leaped down, unfurling his towering form to its full six foot and some inches.

Then he reached his hand inside. She studied his long, olive-hued fingers. Unashamedly naked and desperately requiring gloves, and yet it would be the greatest shame for a scrap of fabric to shield the power of that—"Lady Imogen, do you intend to stand there all day gawking at my hand or . . ."

She slid her fingers into his. Alex wrapped his hand about hers. A heated charge seared through her gloves and burned her skin. Heart thudding loudly in her ears, she stumbled away from him, panicked.

"Come along then," Chloe called out cheerily, motioning her ahead.

Imogen ducked her head and slipped past Alexander. There was an inherent weakness in her. There was no other accounting for this awareness of Lord Alex as a man. Not when the only details she should note of him were his shockingly ill manners, and his hard smile, and his deliberate taunting . . .

Chloe stopped outside a milliner's shop, eying the building a moment. "We shall begin here." With a whir of skirts, she pulled the door open and hurried inside.

In a desperate bid for control, Imogen rushed after Chloe. As she stepped into the shop, Imogen's skin prickled from the awareness of Alex's stare trained on her person. An almost physical urge possessed her to steal one last glance at the chiseled perfection of his high cheeks, his noble brow. She gave her head a clearing shake and stepped deeper into the shop. Wetting her lips, she cast a quick glance about for gossiping ladies who'd delight in being the first to see the shamed Lady Imogen Moore out in Society once more.

The milliner rushed forward, a smile on the plump, older woman's wrinkled cheeks. "May I be of assistance?"

An almost giddy relief filled her at being spared the *ton*'s undue notice. "No, thank you," she murmured. There would be a good deal of cruel whispers and mocking stares to come later, but now she would steal these moments of solitude where she could.

As the woman assisted Chloe, Imogen wandered about the perimeter of the shop. She picked her way around the high wood table littered with fabrics. Ribbons hung down in a rainbow of color from the low ceiling and she trailed her fingers over the soft, satiny fripperies. The gossip would, of course, come. Likely the *ton* even now eagerly anticipated that first function attended by the Moore ladies; one now a beloved duchess, the other . . . well, her. Imogen's stomach tightened with dread. She knew what Chloe sought to do, sparing her the unpleasant business of being with her own family, and appreciated it. She truly did. But Chloe would not always be there and when she wasn't—

A tall figure stepped into her path and she gasped. Lord Alex's well-muscled frame prevented all forward movement. "Lord Alex," she said, her heart quickening in that odd way. His thick black lashes obscured his eyes, giving little indication to what the practiced rogue thought.

"You enjoy shopping." There was a mocking edge to words that were more a statement than anything else.

"No, I quite detest it." She fiddled with a scrap of blue-green satin fabric upon the table, rubbing it between her thumb and forefinger. Alex followed the distracted movement with his hooded eyes. She'd not thought it possible but those thick, black-lashed eyes narrowed further. Unnerved, Imogen dropped the scrap.

"My sister indicated that this shopping trip was at your bequest."

She'd hardly humble herself in giving him the likely truth of Chloe's efforts. "To counter such a claim would require I call Chloe a liar. Which I will not do." She made to step around him.

Alex blocked her path. She gritted her teeth and craned her neck back to meet his gaze. "Is there something else you'd require, Lord Alex?"

He passed his gaze over her face and that foolish organ in her chest thumped that annoying, erratic rhythm. "Do you know, there is," he said on a silken whisper. *Move away*. Instead, she remained fixed to the floor as Alex dipped his head. His breath fanned her lips, the faintest hint of mint and brandy filling her senses, intoxicating in its potency.

Imogen gripped the edge of the table, wanting her words to come out cool and unaffected. "I-is there?" Instead, they emerged with such hesitancy, she damned him and his unflappable, roguish charm.

His hard lips turned up in a mirthless grin. "You *really* don't like me, do you, sweet Imogen?"

It was not a matter of liking him or disliking him, but rather despising the havoc he'd wrought upon her world. She cleared her throat and cast a look about. Chloe and the milliner stood at the front of the shop engrossed in conversation.

The older woman occasionally held up a strip of fabric and Chloe periodically shook her head.

Alex caught the loose strand of hair, draped over Imogen's shoulder by her maid earlier that morning. "Your silence is your answer," he whispered.

Imogen backed up a step, forcing him to release the lock. "I don't know you," she said when she trusted herself to speak, "but for what I've read in the gossip columns." None of which endeared him in any way to a lady who'd had her heart broken by a scoundrel with a glib tongue, who'd charmed Society with the same ease as da Vinci with a brush and easel.

His eyebrows dipped. "And you place a good deal of faith in those gossip sheets, my lady?"

She winced. Touché. Yet she'd not allow him to bully her. "Are the rumors, where you're concerned, false then, Alex?" His body stiffened at her use of his Christian name. Good, with the way he delighted in unnerving her, she rather enjoyed the idea that she'd shocked him. "Are you not a rogue? Do you not . . ." Her skin warmed, but she forced herself to boldly continue. "Earn the hearts of countless widows and married women?"

He strolled over with a languid grace, closing the safe distance she'd put between them. "You would be wrong, Imogen."

"I would?" The whispery-soft quality of her voice may as well have belonged to another. With the slight indent in his squared chin, no gentleman had a right to look so sinfully hard and yet approachable all at the same time.

"Undoubtedly," he continued. He slowly reached an arm out and her breath caught, but he merely picked up a satin strip of yellow fabric on the table behind her. "I do not earn the hearts of those ladies." Alex dropped his voice to a hushed whisper that barely reached her ears. "I earn a place in their beds. Two very entirely different things."

Heat coursed through her body at the shocking admission and she gave a quick prayer of thanks for the jingle of the bell at the front of the shop that jerked his attention away from her. Coward that she was, she slipped past him and continued down the aisle.

A gentleman with Alex's mellifluous tone and seductive looks posed nothing but danger and after the Duke of Montrose's betrayal, Imogen was quite content with a staid, dull gentleman who didn't rouse any sentiments but affection.

With the thrill of awareness that coursed through her every time Alex was near, there was nothing staid or dull about him . . . and all the more reason to avoid him.

For not once in all of the duke's courtship had she felt even the remote stirrings deep inside that she did with a mere grin from Alex. She swallowed hard. With his seductive glances and keen wit, the rakish Lord Alex Edgerton posed more of a danger to her senses than Montrose ever had.

Chapter 5

*T*he ladies, of indeterminate years, were staring quite boldly and unapologetically at Imogen. Such a detail shouldn't have captured his notice, nor should he care. The dark-haired woman in her pale-blue skirts said something to her friend and they erupted into a flurry of giggles. He found Imogen with his gaze.

She stood in the corner of the shop, her back presented to her audience while inspecting a piece of Italian lace. With the young lady's proudly squared shoulders, she gave little indication she'd noted the whispers directed her way. Most ladies would have dissolved into a fit of tears at being so blatantly gossiped about or, in the very least, fled. Respect filled him at the young woman's courage. Then her long, graceful fingers holding the ivory fabric trembled, the slightest hint of Imogen's disquiet.

He did care.

His body jerked erect and he didn't know how to account for this fury on the lady's behalf. The goings-on of young women and how they felt or thought did not affect him, and most certainly not those young women who were friends of his sister.

Another round of too-loud whispers, followed by giggles. Except he'd been victim to another person's abuse, both verbal and physical. He'd not tolerate a woman of Imogen's pride and strength to be so demeaned before the vicious women.

He silently cursed and stalked over to her, ignoring the questioning look she shot him. Positioning himself at her shoulder, he glared the two women into terrified silence. They hastily averted their gazes and carried on in the opposite direction of the shop.

Imogen looked from the women, back to him. Her lips parted in surprise as she registered his intervention. "Thank you," she said softly. Gratitude lit her blue eyes and she shone with an ethereal beauty he'd not known in any of those ladies she'd accused him of bedding.

Uncomfortable with her having gleaned the nature of his efforts, Alex opened his mouth to counter her supposition. Instead, he tugged at his cravat, for the first time in his bloody life without words—where a lady was concerned.

She filled the quiet. "I suspect those who've roused the interest in the gossips the way we two have should, at the very least, support one another," she said with a wink.

An unexpected burst of laughter escaped him at the idea that Lady Imogen thought to include herself in the ranks of a notorious, shiftless rogue such as himself. She joined him laughing, her slender shoulders shaking with mirth.

His mirth died. By King George and all his army, when the lady's eyes sparkled with those silvery flecks, they transformed her into someone really quite—beautiful.

Breathtaking. Captivating. He blanched and retreated a step. Mad. He was going mad. There was no other accounting for his sudden awareness of the Lady Imogen.

"My lord?" she asked tentatively, the amusement fading from her eyes.

And God help him if she didn't still possess the ethereal glow that had robbed him of earlier speech and thought.

Alex schooled his features and adopted the indolent mask he'd perfected through the years. "Even with your scandal, Imogen, you still could never be placed into the dark ranks kept by those such as me."

"You either overestimate the extent of your notoriety or underestimate the scandal in being thrown over by one's betrothed." Something in her wry response, an underlying pain, penetrated his awareness—a reminder of his sister's claim about Imogen loving that lackwit, Montrose.

There, in the middle of the shop, he wanted to tell her that Montrose was a damned, foppish fool she was better off without. But for his title, there was little else to recommend the man. Alex bit back a curse. He had little interest in seeing after the happiness of any other person, his brother's charge of yesterday ringing true. Only . . . Alex couldn't even find happiness for himself, let alone this sometimes tart, often-times cheeky, but always intriguing unwed lady.

"Have you finished?" Chloe hurried over, sparing him from formulating a response and from his own tumultuous thoughts.

Pink stained Imogen's cheeks and she gave a nod, rushing over to meet his sister. "Yes. I have."

Chloe proceeded to prattle on and on, enough for both of the ladies. Arm in arm, she guided Imogen from the shop. Alex trailed behind them at a safe, sizeable distance. He didn't need the complication of looking after Imogen. The lady was not his responsibility. He'd been charged with chaperoning Chloe. Who gave Imogen the cut direct was not his business, nor his concern. So why, in that shop, had he, Alex Edgerton, who lived for his own pleasures, as so correctly accused by his brother yesterday morn, wanted to lash at the lords and ladies who'd thumb their noses at Imogen?

He studied her as she picked her way down the crowded London street. Occasionally, the lady lifted the edge of her skirts and carefully stepped over a muddied puddle. With a rogue's eye he looked forward to those slight, tantalizing moments when he glimpsed the trim ankles. Alex groaned. Lusting after a glimpse of Imogen's skin, he was desperately in need of a visit to Forbidden Pleasures.

A figure stepped into the ladies' path. Imogen's startled gasp cut into the noisy street sounds as the gentleman inadvertently sent her sprawling upon her bottom.

With a curse, he shouldered his way past the colorful dandies and young ladies and came to a stop, prepared to berate the gentleman for his carelessness, but blinked in surprise. The stinging words died on his lips as he recognized Lord Primly. Perhaps the nicest, most harmless chap in all of London.

"E-Edgerton," the man greeted.

The two had attended Eton and Oxford together in the same years. "Primly," he returned.

The tall, slender gentleman in a pea-green jacket looked from Imogen to Alex, his lips parted in horror. "S-so sorry, Edgerton." A dull flush stained his cheeks.

Long ago he'd developed a kind of sympathy for the always-uncomfortable earl. Likely because Alex himself had borne the shame visited upon him by his own father. "All an accident," he said reassuringly. Alex reached past him to help Imogen up. Even through the fabric of her gloves, a surge of heated awareness burned his palm.

Primly spoke, recalling him to the moment. "Quite in b-bad form to b-bowl d-down your sister."

Alex and Imogen spoke in unison.

"She is not my sister."

"He is not my brother."

At the emphatic exclamations, the gentleman scratched his brow as though he was trying to sort through the possible connection between the notorious Lord Alex and the modestly attired young lady. He moved his perplexed blue-eyed gaze back and forth between them.

"I am," Chloe said with a cheerful wave. "The sister, that is. Well, one of them."

Primly screwed his face up in confusion.

Though they moved in vastly different social circles, Alex had always felt sympathy for the man who'd known the scorn and derision showered by the worthless boys at university on him for his stammer. "Allow me to perform introductions," he said to relieve the gentleman of some of his common discomfort. "Primly, my sister, Lady Chloe." Then he stilled as a logical idea slipped into his mind. Primly, as an earl of twenty-eight or twenty-nine years, was most assuredly in the market for a wife. A decent fellow, harmless; the staid gentleman would make Chloe a perfect match. Hell, he would make any lady a perfect match.

With a quick, juddering movement, Primly dipped a bow. "It is an h-honor to m-meet any of Lord Alex's kin." Of course! He was the perfect, un-rogue-like type *any* brother would see his sister wed.

"It is a pleasure, my lord." His sister, however, stole a quick glance longingly down the street, with far less enthusiasm for the potential suitor.

Primly turned his attention to Imogen. A flare of interest, not at all Primly-like, glinted in his eyes. Alex frowned. There was nothing at all *harmless* in the unbridled appreciation in the other man's gaze. The earl looked to him expectantly.

He scowled. Did Primly expect an introduction to the spirited Lady Imogen, whose lips had been made for kissing?

Clearly having tired for the proper introductions to be made, Imogen said, "Hullo." Then she smiled. A smile that, by Alex's way of thinking, was entirely too bright and would only serve to fuel poor Primly's appreciation, which was really not well-done of the lady.

The unassuming young earl fixed a hapless grin on her. Stars may as well have lit the man's eyes.

Oh, bloody hell, he'd had quite enough. The lady really had no business smiling in that—Chloe nudged him with her elbow. He grunted. "Pardon me. Primly, allow me to present Lady Imogen Moore."

Red suffused Primly's pale cheeks as he boldly studied the young lady. And Primly never did anything boldly. Not even say his own name. "My lady. I'm honored t-to make your acquaintance." He sketched a bow and the book tucked under his arm fell to the ground. "F-forgive me." He stooped to retrieve the volume. "I-I was just at the bookshop." Then, brandishing his recent purchase like a knight wielding his broadsword in battle, he waved it about. "Sh-Shakespeare's collection of s-sonnets. I-I'd not been able to find this one for my collection." With his free hand, he pulled at his cravat.

"You read Shakespeare?" The question burst from Imogen's lips.

Was it really so much of a surprise that a gentleman might enjoy Shakespeare's works?

Primly blinked. "I do. N-not that gentlemen are often readers of," his blush deepened, "poetry." He was wrong. Alex himself had long been a devotee of the master playwright.

Chloe laughed. "Imogen is also an ardent admirer of Shakespeare's works."

Alex furrowed his brow. He'd not known that about the lady. Why hadn't he known that? Why would he have *wanted* to know that? Perhaps, because until this very shopping trip, he'd assumed the lady would be more interested in a scrap of fabric than a Shakespearean sonnet.

The ladies favored Primly with matching smiles, as though he were some beloved house pup. "Do you have a favorite work, my lord?" Imogen asked with eagerness in her tone.

His eyes lit under her attention. Once again he waved about his book. "*Hamlet,*" he blurted.

"Ah, *Hamlet*. A wonderful play." She leaned close and lowered her voice, effectively omitting Alex from their exchange. "My favorite character of that play is Polonius, second-in-command, underestimated by all when he is, in fact, a man to be admired, revered, and respected."

Alex might have demonstrated a rotten run of luck at the gaming tables, but he'd wager anything and everything to his name that Primly fell a little bit in love with Imogen just then. A dark niggling that felt a good deal like jealousy stirred in his chest. It was irrational and made little sense and yet it was there, real, with a potent, life-like energy. "Well," he said with forced joviality. "We should be leaving." He didn't know how to account for this desire to spirit Imogen off and keep her to himself.

Primly started. "E-er right, right." He tipped his hat. "F-forgive me," the ever-apologetic nobleman stammered. Then, in an amazing show of fortitude, he captured Imogen's hand. "'Good-bye, good-bye, parting is such great sorrow.'"

Oh, for the love of King George and all the king's men. *Goodnight.*

A little sigh escaped Imogen's lips. Over Primly and an incorrect verse? Alex gritted his teeth. "Goodnight," he snapped. The trio looked to him as though he'd sprung a second head. *Shut your blasted mouth.* "The verse is in fact 'Goodnight, goodnight. Parting is such sweet sorrow.'" An awkward silence met his pronouncement. A dull flush climbed up his neck. "It just seemed important that . . . you know," he finished lamely.

As though startled into recalling propriety, Primly released Imogen's long, graceful fingers. "Er, uh, of course," Primly said, tugging at his ear. "E-Edgerton, a pleasure as always. Lady Imogen, Lady Chloe." He sketched another bow and then at last took his leave.

The ladies dropped curtsies, then hurried ahead in the opposite direction. "That was rather rude of you," Chloe chided.

Yes, it had been. Primly was actually the opposite of the condescending, self-serving lords he'd come to detest through the years. Something about the man's interest in Imogen had roused this unholy annoyance in his chest. He didn't care to think about why it was he'd wanted to separate Primly's hand from his person for having touched her gloved fingertips. Alex was not a gentleman to be roused to jealousy and most assuredly not over a young lady in the market for a husband. Why, Primly was a perfectly suitable match for her and . . . That haze of red descended over his vision once more.

He blinked several times and then when he opened his eyes, he found Imogen missing. Alex stopped midstride and whirled about, searching for the fiery-haired beauty and his sister, and then his gaze landed upon the two ladies outside the entrance of The Temple of the Muses. The building, several stories tall, opened some years back by James Lackington, offered all manner of books for purchase.

Alex strode back down the cobblestone and reached the front of the establishment just as Chloe pressed the door handle and slipped inside. He spoke, staying Imogen. "You enjoy reading, do you, Imogen?"

"Yes." She paused and looked up at him. "Does that surprise you?" A challenge lit her eyes.

Alex motioned her forward. "Actually, yes," he murmured as she stepped inside. He paused a moment to admire the graceful swell of her buttocks. "Most women would rather spend their days at the hosier or milliner than in a bookshop."

Chloe made her way up the stairs at the back left corner. More than expecting her to bolt after his sister, Imogen shocked him by slowing her steps and allowing him to walk beside her. "You do not have a high opinion of those belonging to the opposite sex, do you?"

"I've been given little reason to trust a lady's motives. My experience has shown them to be self-serving and greedy." His words earned a small frown from the young lady. There had been scores of debutantes who'd not had a glance for the second-born son. "So you are indeed correct. I do not hold your sex in a favorable opinion."

Imogen wagged an eyebrow. "Then perhaps you are keeping company with the wrong ladies, Lord Alex." With that, she walked down the aisle, trailing her fingers over the leather volumes.

Alex cast a glance over his shoulder. He'd been tasked with the responsibility of seeing to Chloe. He should follow after his young, prone-to-mischief sister . . . and yet, with the graceful sway of her hips, Imogen was a siren. The manner in which she ran distracted fingers over the leather books drew him forth. He pursued her. "And who are the correct ladies?"

His quietly spoken question brought her to a stop. Imogen turned slightly, her gaze trained on the books before her. "Certainly not those scandalous ladies you spoke of earlier," she chided. With hands that had haunted his waking and sleeping thoughts since yesterday morn, she plucked a copy of *Hamlet* from the shelf, reminding him of her words for Primly. She fanned the pages of the leather volume. "The ones who have little interest in your heart." Did she even now think of the other man?

He tightened his jaw. "I do not have a heart."

She furrowed her brow. "Everyone has a heart, Alex." She gave him a sad look. "You may have forgotten how to use it because it's been so hurt, but it is there and someday you will find the person who teaches that organ to again beat."

Her words ran through him with a shocking intimacy that caused his heart to thud in a panicked rhythm. He forced a casual grin and took another step toward her. Then another. Until just the span of a palm separated them, close enough that the fragrant hint of lemon that clung to her skin wrapped about his senses. He lowered his lips close to her ear. "You presume much, Imogen." Alex captured her artfully arranged curl. The maid who'd done this work should be sacked for the tantalizing creature she'd set out into Society. "Perhaps you should place more credence in those scandal sheets you so abhor." Unable to resist the lure of that strand, he raised the silken tress to his nose and inhaled the citrusy scent of lemon.

The book in her fingers tumbled to the floor at their feet, forgotten. "I-I won't do that," she stammered, her fiery lashes fluttering wildly.

He reveled in the subtle movement that spoke to her desire. "I don't believe in love. I believe in cold practicality and reason. When I desire a woman," she sucked in an audible breath, "I take her, and I worship her with my body. That is the most honest and real emotion that can exist between two people." He hurled those scandalous words at her, in a silent bid to send her fleeing from the shock of them, even as he longed for her to stay just as she was, her body flush against his.

Imogen opened her eyes. Sadness, pity, and desire all swirled within their blue depths. "I fear if you truly believe that, you live a very lonely, sad existence."

Her words struck like an arrow entirely too close to the truths he kept buried, even from himself—until now. "And what of you?" Alex captured her lower lip between his thumb and forefinger and toyed with the plump flesh. "You would have married Montrose, and for what?"

"Do you expect because I was betrothed to an illustrious duke I aspired to a grand title above all else?" She winged a fiery eyebrow upward, giving no indication that mere moments ago she'd been breathless with desire. "Do you believe I didn't love him?"

The muscles of his stomach contracted at the pairing of her, Montrose, and the emotion love. "Don't all ladies?"

"No, they don't." She cupped his cheek. "That *is* what you believe, isn't it?" she asked softly. "That ladies merely desire a titled lord?"

A muscle jumped at the corner of his mouth. From her gentle caress? His own turbulent thoughts? "That is the truth." He spoke with the conviction that came of experience in being that lord desired for nothing more than the pleasure he could give a lady when she was properly wed.

"Oh, Alex, that is not the truth." Her arm fell back to her side and he damned the loss of her gentle touch. "I didn't want William for his title." *William*. Something primitive stirred in his chest at her use of the duke's Christian name. That familiarity born of two people who'd been betrothed and very nearly married. She dropped her gaze to his cravat. "I wanted him because I loved him, or I thought I did," she murmured, more to herself.

Just then, Alex hated the Duke of Montrose. Hated him for reasons he did not understand, and reasons he couldn't put to rights with Imogen so very close. "But you were lured by his title," he said, desperately needing to consign her to the place of fortune-hunting misses where she was far safer to his senses.

For a moment, she touched her fingers to the pendant she wore about her neck and then she let her hands fall back to her side. "I was attracted to him because he made me laugh." Her eyes grew distant and the familiar loathing burned in his gut at the man who occupied her memories. "He saw past my scandal." There had been a scandal? She'd have her third Season and he himself had only just noticed her now. "He didn't care about Society's ill-opinion of me when I'd made my Come Out."

And for that she'd rewarded Montrose her heart and the bastard had married her sister. He bit back the scornful words.

"You see, we are not unalike, Alex." They were nothing alike. "You ceased believing in love for reasons I don't know . . ."

He'd ceased believing at the hand of his father, the person who should have loved him unconditionally and who instead taught him that love, in fact, had conditions. From early on, Alex came to appreciate that the sentiment merely weakened one. He would not make himself victim to anyone else.

The weak fool he'd once been had died with his bastard of a father. "And you ceased because your betrothed wed your sister," he said with a bluntness that made her flinch.

She managed a jerky nod. "Yes." Imogen raised her eyes to his. "Only, I didn't truly cease believing in love." Emotion lit the blues of her eyes. "Or hoping for it, for myself."

Ah, God, this was dangerous. These were wishes, desires, and dreams he knew nothing about and had studiously avoided. Until now. Alex cupped his palm around the nape of her neck and angled her closer. "Montrose was a bloody fool," he whispered and there, with but the risk of a patron passing by away from ruin, he kissed her.

Imogen stiffened and then almost instantly her body turned soft and pliant in his arms. He slanted his mouth over hers, tasting the lush contours of a mouth made for sin, desired since he'd stepped into the library yesterday morn. She wrapped her hands about his neck and twined them in his hair.

With a barely suppressed groan, he slipped his tongue inside her mouth and delved deep. She tasted of honey and mint and he reveled in the sweet, intoxicating blend. Imogen boldly met his tongue in a thrust and parry. The desire to have her laid out before him hit him with a staggering intensity.

It isn't enough.

He ran his hands down her back, over the curve of her hip, collecting her buttocks. He dragged her close against his straining flesh. She moaned and he swallowed it, the sound vibrating in his mouth.

A loud thump sounded from somewhere down one of the aisles.

Alex jerked his head up. His heart thundered with the intensity of his own desire. Horror replaced the thick fog of desire in Imogen's eyes as she glanced about. She touched a hand to the mussed curls. Silently, he turned her around and set to work tucking the handful of loose curls back into the butterfly combs at the base of her head. "Go," he whispered against her ear, drawing in the intoxicating scent of her once more. "Or I won't stop at a mere kiss in the future, Imogen."

She took off at a near run down the aisle, as though the hounds of hell nipped at her heels where she promptly collided with Chloe.

"There you are," Chloe exclaimed, catching Imogen about the shoulders. "Have you finished your shopping?"

Imogen's murmured response was lost to him.

Chloe beamed. "Splendid!" With a flick of her wrist, his sister beckoned him over. "Come along, Alex, it is time to seek out the carriage."

Alex scrubbed a hand over his eyes. A closed carriage ride with Lady Imogen Moore, who in the span of a damned afternoon had upended his thoughts?

Bloody hell.

Chapter 6

*I*mogen sat at the edge of her bed. She fiddled with the silly pendant her friend had put about her neck more than a week ago. Seven days had passed since Alex's bold, unrepentant kiss and the stilted carriage ride to follow. In that time, she and Chloe had been to Egyptian Hall, and shopping down Bond Street, and for a stroll through Hyde Park. Through each outing, they'd been accompanied by the roguish Lord Alex. In all those times, he'd been perfectly polite and surprisingly proper. In short, the perfect chaperone . . . so much so that she began to wonder if she'd merely *imagined* that kiss.

Her thoughts continued to stray back to The Temple of the Muses. With Alex's huskily spoken words and the promise in his eyes, he'd robbed her of logic and wrought havoc upon her senses.

No. Lord Alex Edgerton, rake of the worst sort, a nonbeliever in love, with his cynical smile and mellifluous baritone, had kissed her and that embrace had been very real. She pressed her eyes closed. God help her, for she'd wanted him to continue doing so. Had wanted it with such an intensity that her body still burned with remembrance of his touch, the feel of him pressed against her belly.

He, on the other hand, gave little indication that he'd felt . . . well, anything. She scoffed. What would he feel? Even as Alex's kiss had burned a mark upon her soul, a man who took his pleasures where he willed likely remained unmoved by that exchange.

Imogen hid her face into her palms and buried a groan as she remembered how she'd moaned and whimpered into his mouth like one of those . . . those . . . shameful ladies he spoke unrepentantly of. She could count on three fingers of one hand the number of times William, the Duke of Montrose, had kissed her. Two of those kisses had been upon the right cheek, but one had involved a meeting of their mouths. His fetid breath and soft lips had never, ever roused that dangerous emotion of desire in her belly, liquefying her until her body ran hot on the inside and out.

The door opened and she jerked her head up. Her mother slipped into her chambers. "Mother," she greeted, climbing to her feet. Could her mother see the guilt of her thoughts stamped upon her face?

Mother closed the door behind her. "Surely you know you cannot avoid your sister and her husband forever."

The memory of Alex's touch went cold. "I know," she said. She eyed the clock in the corner of the room. Her mother would not relent until this very public, first exchange between enemy sisters and the duke who'd chosen one and wed the other, had taken place.

"Your sister and His Grace will be at the Williston Ball this evening." She pursed her lips. "I had hoped you would come."

Of course she had. She foolishly believed that once the sisters' reunion occurred, Society would then shift their attention to some other poor, unsuspecting young lady.

"I was invited to the theater by Chloe." Chloe could have invited her to dine with the devil in hell that evening and Imogen would have taken that option over seeing her sister and brother-in-law. She smoothed her skirts. "She will likely arrive any moment and I should be—"

Mother held a palm up, silencing her. "I do so want you to be as happy as your sister is with Montrose." Odd, Imogen had hung so much of her happiness on that match and broken betrothal, she expected her mother's words should hurt more. "I've accepted the invitation to Lady Ferguson's ball later this week. Your sister will be there." Imogen sprung forward on the balls of her feet, prepared to launch her whole self into her argument. "And you are going." Her mother's throat moved. "It breaks my heart to see you hurting as you are."

Imogen cocked her head. Odd, she'd been consumed by a misery of her sister's making for so very long. Only at this moment, she realized she'd not really spared one resentful thought of either Rosalind or Montrose since Alex had made it a point of teasing her and talking to her . . . and kissing her.

"Are you listening to me, Imogen?"

She started. "Er, yes," she lied, thrusting aside the jumbled musings of Alex. Imogen nodded. "I know you want me to be happy and I will be." Before her mother could say anything further, Imogen leaned over and kissed her on the cheek. "If you'll excuse me, Chloe should arrive any moment." Her friend should have arrived more than ten minutes ago. Alas, she'd learned long ago how dismal Chloe was in matters of timing.

"Oh, and Imogen?"

She paused, fingers on the door handle.

"There is nothing shameful in having a marquess for a husband." Imogen stiffened and, as though she couldn't make sense of that less than subtle hint, her mother said, "The Marquess of Waverly would make you a splendid match."

A splendid match. She may as well have spoken of fabrics being paired together. Imogen pulled the door open and made her way from the room and through the long corridors. Her mother's grasping words echoed around the chambers of her mind, blurring with Alex's earlier charge.

But you were lured by his title . . .

She frowned, secretly acknowledging his charged accusations about most women and their title grasping as fact. Was it any wonder he had such a low opinion of ladies? For the first time, she considered Lord Alex Edgerton not as the cynical rake, but rather as the man he'd been before. Imogen turned at the end of the hall and, running her fingers over the banister, she descended the white Italian marble staircase.

The butler stood in wait at the bottom, her emerald cloak held out.

She slipped into it. "Thank you, Masterson."

"Lady Imogen," he murmured, and then quickly pulled the door open. "Lady Chloe's carriage arrived a short while ago." He glanced pointedly beyond her shoulder.

"Thank you," she mouthed, knowing Mother even now likely trailed after her. She stepped outside, the cool night air caressed her face and she embraced the momentary freedom, away from the talk of Rosalind and the duke or Mother and her hopes for Imogen. Any of it and all of it.

With a spring in her step, she made her way over to the Marquess of Waverly's waiting carriage. A liveried footman stood, arms clasped behind him, beside the black lacquer barouche.

From within the elegant carriage, Chloe peeked from behind the red velvet curtain, a wide smile on her plump, ivory cheeks, and waved.

Imogen eagerly returned the gesture and rushed the remaining steps to the carriage.

The servant pulled the door open and helped hand her up. Her eyes struggled to adjust to the dark confines of the marquess's carriage. "Thank . . ." her gaze collided with Alexander's. Her heart sped up. ". . . you," she whispered.

"Indeed, Imogen," he drawled. Alexander beat his palm upon his thick, well-muscled thigh.

Her cheeks warmed and she yanked her gaze up to find him studying her through thick black lashes. "L-Lord Alex. Chloe," she greeted. His indolent tone and the hard glint in his eyes indicated he'd spent a good deal less time than she in thinking of their passionate exchange. Against the bookshelves. With his mouth on hers. His tongue touching hers.

Alexander held her stare. "Never tell me you were again expecting the marquess?"

Actually, yes, yes she had been. As had her mother. She bit the inside of her cheek to keep from saying as much and hurried to claim the seat alongside Chloe. She hardly believed her mother would look as favorably upon a trip to the theater with Chloe's scandalous other brother.

"Do forgive my brother," Chloe said, making apologies for the jaded rogue. "I swear he's been in a foul mood since we visited The Temple of the Muses last week."

Imogen's heart started. "Has he?" she asked softly. In all their meetings since that day, he'd been the perfectly charming, polite brother. She stole another look at Alex, but the harsh, angular planes of his face may as well have been carved from stone for all the emotion she could decipher.

He remained stonily silent.

"Oh, yes," Chloe said with a nod. "Grumbling and grousing all day, every day since."

Imogen rushed to contribute something to a conversation. "Did you not enjoy yourself that afternoon, Lord Alex?"

A sound, half groan, half laugh rumbled from his chest and Imogen's whole body heated with the shame of that unintended question. "I assure you, I did quite enjoy that *afternoon*, my lady," he said, his tone guttural and rough. "It was very pleasurable." He shifted his leg, so his knee pressed against hers. "And tell me, Imogen, did you enjoy yourself?"

More than she had in the three Seasons she'd been in London. Imogen's mouth went dry in remembrance of his kiss and she allowed her gaze to linger upon him, the hard chiseled planes of his face, the slight cleft in his chin. Her breath caught at the hot stare he had trained on her.

Chloe elbowed her in the side. "You mustn't be fooled by his attempt to charm you." She dropped her voice to a not-so-soft whisper. "Alex is still surly at being forced to carry on as chaperone instead of visiting one of his fancy pieces."

The muscles of Imogen's stomach tightened at the much needed, unwitting reminder given by her friend.

"Chloe," Alexander said sharply. "That is enough."

His sister had apparently grown immune to her older brother's displeasure. "You needn't be so stodgy, isn't that right, Imogen? We are both quite informed about your—"

"Chloe," he snapped.

Her friend went wide-eyed, likely unaccustomed to be spoken to so harshly by her affable, charming-to-everyone-except-Imogen brother.

Imogen pressed herself against the side of the carriage. Feeling his gaze on her, she shifted the curtain and peered at the passing dark, London streets. Alexander might set her heart aflutter and send heat coursing through her body, but he was a rogue and she'd have a gentleman who was constant or no one at all.

A man such as him would kiss a lady in one moment and forget her name in the next. To believe she was, or could ever be, something more to a man of Lord Alex Edgerton's reputation would be the height of foolishness from one determined to never make a fool of herself where love was concerned—not again. Yet, the more time she spent in Alex's presence, the more he threw her senses into an upheaval.

A relieved sigh slipped past her lips as the marquess's carriage rocked to a stop at the front of the theater.

Suddenly, when presented with the possibility of spending the evening with Alexander inside his private box, with him wreaking havoc on her emotions, she found she rather preferred the safety in that first meeting with her sister and brother-in-law to the uncertainty of being alone with a hopeless rogue like Lord Alex Edgerton.

As Alex trailed behind his sister and Imogen, he seethed with annoyance. Chloe, with her casual speech, had painted him in the most unfavorable of light to Imogen. The lady thought him a rake who took his pleasure where he would and then moved on to the next warm, eager body . . .

He paused at the entrance of the theater and stood staring at Imogen's back. Isn't that what he was? Isn't that the man he'd been so many years he didn't believe he could be or wanted to be anyone but that man? Yet, he loathed that Imogen should look at him with a very mature, cynical glint in her blue eyes. Instead, he preferred her as she'd been against the shelving of books: hot, moaning, desperate for him. But then, it was all the other emotions he didn't know what to do with. Passion, he'd always been comfortable with.

Alex gave his head a shake and forced himself to continue walking. He strode inside the theater, quickly locating the pair of young ladies. They stood facing one another, their heads close as they conspired together. He groaned, as all the reservations in being charged the task of looking after his headstrong, often-inappropriate-for-a-young-lady sister surfaced. The loud din of guests' chatter proved nearly deafening. He worked his way through the crush of bodies, his gaze trained on an easy-to-identify pile of fiery tresses, locks that had been set ablaze by the sun. He recoiled. Bloody hell, what was the matter with him?

A tall figure stepped into his path.

He cursed. "Bloody . . ." The world trailed off. "Stanhope," he said blankly, staring at his recently married friend and the other man's wife, the Lady Anne. Their friendship went back to their days at Eton, a close bond only strengthened when Alex had served as the other man's second upon a dueling field many, many years go. He stole a glance about for Chloe and Imogen. "Bloody hell." The crowd of bodies had swallowed them.

"A pleasure to see you, as well." Stanhope grinned. "I daresay I never believed I'd see the day you'd be spending your evenings at the theater."

Yes, they two had made it a habit of visiting gaming hells and some of the more disreputable clubs. Until the other man had wed, leaving Alex to his own lonely carousing.

"Oh, hush," Lady Anne said, peering at the chandelier overhead. She turned her attention to Alex. "It is a pleasure to see you," she said with a smile while making the proper greetings.

Alex sketched a belated bow. "Lady Stanhope," he said with an almost pained discomfort. "The pleasure is all mine." When presented with his friend's unexpected interest in the lady some months past, he'd made no secret his dislike for the woman rumored to be a title-grasping, self-indulgent miss. Just as all the others of the peerage . . .

That is what you believe, isn't it? That a lady merely desires a titled lord . . . ?

With a silent curse, he glanced about for Imogen. Rather, his sister. He searched for . . .

"Are you searching for someone?" Stanhope drawled.

"Yes," he muttered, searching for crimson curls. Only because it was far easier to identify the flaming locks amidst a sea of pale blonde and not because he was in any way captivated by the chit.

"And do you care to mention who it is you are in fact—?"

"Oh, shove off, Stanhope. It is my sister," he gritted out.

The other man tossed his head back on a laugh. "By God, I never thought I'd see the day." Anxiety roiled through him, the fear of his own transparency to this friend who knew him too well. "You are a chaperone?" Some of the tension left his frame at his friend's erroneous assumption about his disquiet.

"Yes," he bit out. And he'd gone and lost her and Imogen. "A charge doled out by my brother, the illustrious marquess."

A somberness replaced Stanhope's earlier amusement. "Ah, I see." This man was the only one who knew a piece of the hell Alexander had lived as a child, and the bond he'd shared with Gabriel that had been severed by his father's manipulations. His friend searched about the hall. "I believe I see her, alongside the column just to the right of the doors. She is with a young lady and Lord Primly—" Goddamn

Primly. "Where are you go—?" Stanhope called after him, but Alex continued moving.

He pressed ahead through the crowd, shouldering his way past gentlemen calling out a greeting. Only one gentleman had his notice this instant. He narrowed his eyes on the slender gentleman in a burnt-orange satin jacket to rival the hue of Imogen's tresses. Every so often, Primly dropped his gaze to her delectable décolletage.

Something tightened in Alex's belly, unpleasant and gripping, something that, had he been anyone other than his jaded, cynical self, he would have believed was jealousy. Which was madness—to be jealous of unassuming Primly—who continued to ogle the creamy white skin exposed above the lace trim of her gown. "Primly," he snapped, as he came upon them.

The other man glanced up, flushing guiltily. "Er . . . E-Edgerton. A-a pleasure, I-I was j-just—"

Alex leveled the man with a glower until Primly backed away, his cheeks white. He'd known very well what the illustrious young earl had been doing.

"Poor Lord Primly," his sister said with stern reproach. "You are quite horrid to the gentleman."

He gritted his teeth. "May we find our seats?" With that he turned on his heel and guided them through the crowd to their respective box.

Chloe slid into a red velvet armchair and perched herself on the edge. She proceeded to boldly study those filing into their seats.

Imogen shifted back and forth on her feet, studiously avoiding his gaze, avoiding it when she'd held Primly's and offered the bastard a smile and—

"Sit, Imogen."

She froze and looked up at him. "I beg your pardon?"

Heat burned his neck and he resisted the urge to tug at his cravat.

"I am not one of your hunting dogs, Lord Alex. I—"

"I don't have hunting dogs. Now, will you please sit? You are, *we* are," he amended, "attracting notice."

Her gaze flew out toward the theater. A sea of curious stares was trained upon the scandalous Lady Imogen Moore, nearly left at the altar for her sister. She blanched. With swift, jerky movements, she claimed a seat. He searched for a hint of her weakening in front of the merciless *ton*. Instead, Imogen remained poised as a queen, her chin tipped up, and a defiant glint in her eyes. Most other women would have dissolved into a fit of tears before the scorn now bestowed upon her. Just then, Imogen rose even higher in his esteem.

Alex settled into the chair beside her, so close his leg brushed hers. The subtle movement was made all the more heady by the citrusy scent that clung to her. Did the lady add lemon to her bathwater? Dab it behind her ears? On the heel of such thoughts were imaginings of Imogen, naked, her skin pinkened from the heat of her bathwater.

He drew in a slow, steadying breath as the chore of venturing out into polite Society events became torturous for altogether different reasons that had nothing to do with the role of chaperone.

Alexander was staring at her. Then, nearly every lord and lady within the theater this evening had at some point stolen a glance at the pitiable, scandalous Moore sister. Except . . . Alex's fixed, heated gaze was not the pitying kind. Instead, his nearly jade irises seared her with an intensity rousing wicked thoughts and remembrances of his mouth upon hers.

Imogen closed her eyes and searched for resolve. She would not be weak. She had already been weak where one gentleman was concerned and in that, she'd learned to be wary of a man who stared at a lady as though she were the only woman in the world. When in truth, a rogue such as Alex would never see but one woman. He would take his pleasures where he would and with as many of those ladies who were wholly uninterested in his heart. Pain scissored through her.

> *These violent delights have violent ends*
> *And in their triumph die, like fire and powder . . .*

Imogen touched the cold pendant about her neck, a talisman purported to bring its wearer the heart of a duke, but for her it served as a different reminder—the perils from having loved that duke. That grand sentiment of love so many ladies aspired to but never dared speak aloud, a dream she had allowed herself. She'd not make the same folly twice. Not in giving her attention, her heart, or any part of herself to an unrepentant rogue. When she loved again, it would be with an honorable man who'd respect the gift of her affections and put her before all.

Squaring her jaw, she fixed her attention on the actors below. Some of the tension left her as she allowed herself to become lost in the performance. "'Ay, pilgrim, lips that they must use in prayer,'" she silently mouthed along with the actress on the stage below. The fair Juliet's words an unwitting reminder of Alexander's kiss. She layered her palm against her cheek, hating that a sliver of her soul clung to the romanticism she'd once dreamed of for herself. The young lady who'd attended finishing school had secretly longed for a life upon the stage. The allure of those plays had tantalized a young girl with a romantic spirit.

Alex leaned close. His breath tickled her ear. "'See, how she leans her cheek upon her hand! O, that I were a glove upon that hand, that I might caress that cheek.'"

Her heart fluttered and she dropped her hand to her lap, clutching the fabric. "T-touch," she corrected. "That I m-might touch that cheek."

"Yes, and yet a caress is so much more meaningful than a mere touch, wouldn't you say, Imogen?" Alex slid his gloved hand over hers, staying her distracted movement.

Yes, oh goodness, she quite agreed. His touch coupled with his knowledge of Shakespeare was heady stuff, indeed. "You read Shakespeare," she said, unable to keep the shock from her statement.

He turned on her the very question she'd put to him last week. "Are you surprised?" Suddenly, he stopped that gentle stroking and she mourned the loss of that seductive little movement. She bit the inside of her lip to keep from begging him to continue.

"N-not at all." She *was*, however, surprised he read the romantic words of William Shakespeare. Nor did she care for this side of Alex. This shared love and fascination of the Bard's works that made him more human than rake.

"I find myself surprised by you." He slipped his fingers into hers, intertwining the digits. His hand strong and powerful, hers fragile and delicate against it, and yet somehow perfectly paired. "You intrigue me."

"Why would that be?" Her heart thumped erratically at his touch, his words. With the exception of her broken betrothal and flaming-red hair, nothing had earned the notice of anyone—until Alex. "There is nothing unordinary about me." William's fickle interest had proven testament to that.

"There is everything extraordinary about you," His lips nearly brushed her ear and when he spoke in that husky, mellifluous whisper, she could almost believe it. "You quote Shakespeare, sweet Imogen?" His strong, powerful fingers tightened about hers in a seductively possessive grip.

Here in the midst of polite Society, with a theater full of lords and ladies looking for the next piece of gossip, he'd enthralled her. "I do." Not always intentionally. Imogen swallowed and stole a glance about, but Chloe sat perched at the edge of the box, engrossed in the show below. She looked about the theater. How could anyone not see that with each stroke of his hand over hers, Alex threw her world into greater tumult?

"You hate shopping, but you enjoy the theater." With infinite slowness, he rolled her satin theater glove slowly down her arm and then freed each finger from the restrictive confines. Imogen darted her gaze about. Surely someone knew the seductive game Alex now played. Yet even two seats apart, her friend remained engrossed in the production below. Wholly uncaring of who might observe his bold touch, Alex whispered, "What manner of woman are you?" He rested her glove upon his lap.

She sucked in a breath at his intimate caress. "Wh-what are—?"

"Shh," he whispered. Alex stroked his thumb in small, soothing circles about her palm eliciting all manner of delicious shivers that radiated at the point of contact and spread through her.

Her chest heaved up and down with slow, shallow breaths. His was just a hand and his fingers moved in a really innocuous movement, except . . . Imogen bit her lower lip as he rubbed his thumb over the wildly fluttering pulse at her wrist. The small, seductive grin upon his lips indicated he knew he'd roused her senses.

"Romeo had the wrong of it, Imogen." His husky murmur stirred her belly.

She shouldn't engage in this seductive game with him. It was outrageous and meant nothing to him. "I-in what way do you believe?" She could no sooner quell the question on her lips than she could stop the beating of her own heart.

He studied her through thick black lashes. "I'd not feel your gloved hand upon me. I'd have your naked palm caressing me, touching me."

God forgive her. Her lids fluttered madly. She still was the same weak, romantic fool she'd always been. Alex had only opened her eyes to the passion she carried inside, made all the more dangerous by the shred of hope she clung to—to love and be loved.

I do not have a heart . . .

She met his gaze. He continued to study her in that piercing, penetrating way. As though he knew her secrets and reveled in them. It would be too easy to believe herself in love with him. Only, a man such as he would never turn himself over to love and she would be wise to listen to the mistakes of her past, her not-so-distant past, where Alex was concerned. Imogen plucked her glove from his lap, warmth spiraling through her as her fingers brushed his thigh. She made quick work of tugging it into place, just as Chloe glanced over. Imogen mustered a smile for her friend who grinned in return and looked to the stage once more.

"Tsk, tsk, where is your boldness, Imogen?"

"Buried under my sense of propriety, Lord Alex," she said from the corner of her mouth.

He draped his arm along the top of her chair and leaned back, elegant in repose. "You'd agreed to call me Alexander." His lazy repose would have been casual by any other observer who glanced over this moment, and yet, his well-muscled thigh went taut against hers, speaking to his heightened tension.

She gritted her teeth, hating that she desired him as she did. "I never agreed to call you by your Christian name. I . . ."

He stared expectantly at her.

She'd merely taken to using it at his urging. "Furthermore—"

"You didn't finish the first part of your argument, love."

Love. Ah, what manner of fool was she to crave that endearment upon his lips? He smiled, a knowing grin. The lout. "Furthermore," she repeated on a hushed whisper. "You've quite conveniently forgotten the second part of Mr. Shakespeare's quote."

Alexander sent an eyebrow arching upward.

"'What's in a name? That which we call a rose by any other name would smell as sweet.'" That very important second verse cleverly left out by a lord who'd take pleasures where he would and not give a thought to the heartbreak he left in his wake. She worked her gaze over his face. "What matters is what something is, not what it is called." And he was a rogue. And she was a lady who'd had her heart broken. Even if she wished it, which she assuredly did not, there could be no more imperfect pairing than they two.

Another seductive grin tugged at the corner of his lips. "And I am what? A rogue? A blackhearted scoundrel?" The faint teasing tone to that handful of words was underscored by a steely hardness.

"Isn't that what you claimed just last week, Alex?" she shot back with a question of her own. "To possess no heart."

His body jerked as though she'd struck him. "Indeed, my lady." Those three terse words were more telling than any other he could have strung together.

And there, in the middle of the theater, amidst a sea of lords and ladies, Imogen came to the staggering realization— the cavalier exterior presented to the world by Lord Alex Edgerton was nothing more than a show, not very different than the Drury Lane production even now being performed upon the stage.

His was a craftily sculpted image of an indolent rogue when, in actuality, he desired more, craved more—even as he himself likely didn't know it.

How had she failed to see the carefully presented facade before now? Her heart ached with a desire to tug down all the carefully constructed walls he'd built about him. Imogen slipped her hand over his, expecting she should be beset with terror.

He stiffened and cast his gaze down, meeting her eyes with an unflinching boldness.

Except there was no fear.

For a moment, she suspected he intended to pull away, but then, wordlessly, he placed his other hand atop hers. Imogen's heart spasmed. This was very bad, indeed.

Swallowing past a wave of emotion in her throat, she picked her head up and wished she hadn't. Because if she hadn't looked out across the sea of theatergoers, she wouldn't have seen the notorious, recently widowed Viscountess Kendricks eying Alexander as though he were a savory treat in a world without food. Even with the distance of the theater between them, she detected the glimmer of interest contained within those catlike eyes.

Imogen stole a sideways glance to see if Alex noted the bold widow's sultry movements. He stared directly out across the theater at the dark-haired beauty, his expression inscrutable.

A viselike pressure tightened about her heart as the widow toyed with the fabric of her plunging décolletage. Imogen took in the bold display and then with wooden movements, she withdrew her hand from Alex's. The bold exchange between the notorious Lady Kendricks and the sought-after lord merely served as a much needed reminder—no good could come from caring for one such as him.

Chapter 7

$\mathcal{T}$he following morning, in the privacy of her chambers, Imogen reflected on the roguish, Shakespeare-quoting, Lord Alex. Be they gentlemen or noblemen or servants, all men were the same. Every one of them was attracted to a lovely woman and saw nothing much beyond a superficial beauty. Her first lesson of that fact had been dealt by the powerful Duke of Montrose. And really, no other lessons were required after such a betrayal. Alexander's interest in the stunningly voluptuous Lady Kendricks had only reinforced that now obvious fact.

Standing by the window in her chambers, Imogen turned her attention to the volume of *Romeo and Juliet* in her fingers. Except, all thoughts of Shakespeare's bold, beautiful words and the woes of star-crossed lovers were now a mere shadow to the memory of Alexander's touch last evening, his whispers. With a groan, she tossed the book onto a nearby mahogany side table. It slid off the smooth, mahogany surface and landed on the floor with a loud thump.

What manner of fool was she that she should have had her heart so broken, her trust betrayed by a rogue, and then find herself so completely captivated by another that she'd stand beside a window, like a lovelorn pup, dreaming of him, wishing he could be more, so that mayhap they could be more?

"Enough," she scolded herself. With a determined stride, she marched over to the door and tugged it open. The best way to put the memory of his touch aside was certainly not to remain in the quiet of her chambers, recalling his fingers upon her naked palm. Or . . . Another growl of annoyance climbed up her throat as she stomped along the corridor, detesting her soft, satin slippers that made barely a hint of sound upon the thin, ivory carpet. Imogen reached the staircase and bounded down the steps at an unladylike pace. She reached the bottom and nearly collided with Masterson. A startled gasp escaped her and she pressed a hand to her heart.

"I beg your pardon, my lady." There was something faintly panicky in the furtive manner he darted his gaze about.

She smiled at the usually unflappable servant, who'd long been devoted, stoic, and everything kind. "It is entirely my—"

He held up a folded missive in his gloved hands. "This arrived for you, my lady."

Recognizing Chloe's familiar scrawl, she accepted the note. "Thank you," she said and made to step around him eager to read the letter from her friend.

Masterson repositioned himself, blocking her retreat. "My lady." His voice emerged as a hoarse croak. He stole another glance around, and when he returned his attention to her, his expression was as distressed as one who'd gotten all his toes quite painfully stomped.

And this was a side of poor Masterson she'd not seen. "I assure you, I was not at all startled," she said in a soothing tone. She'd thought he and the other servants had learned long ago she was not one of those screeching, frowning, ladies in the house.

"Her Grace, the Duchess of Montrose, is here," he said on a rush, and then his shoulders drooped as though shamed by his own boldness.

The Duchess of Montrose. She widened her eyes as the implication of those words seeped into her brain. "Oh," she blurted. Imogen eyed the long staircase, contemplating escaping back up to her chambers. Her mother would demand she put in an appearance and then she'd have to see *him*. Odd, she expected she should feel the bitter regret of his betrayal. Instead, she merely felt annoyance at the arrogant, foppish gentleman now married to her sister. She looked to Masterson. "Is—?"

"She's arrived alone," he supplied, saving her the indignity of inquiring after the man she'd been betrothed to. "I showed her to the Blue Parlor a short while ago where she's now taking tea with Her Ladyship."

The faint wave of relief was fleeting. She'd still not see Rosalind. Not now, gloating and triumphant and all things rude and condescending as she'd been throughout their early years and onward. A panicky urge to flee caused her toes to twitch involuntarily. Imogen wet her lips and looked about.

Masterson cleared his throat. "I took the liberty of having the carriage readied, my lady." A footman rushed forward with her cloak.

She furrowed her brow. "Readied . . . ?" she said, more to herself.

"I'd believed you'd asked the carriage readied so you could pay a visit to Lady Chloe."

Visit Chloe. She looked blankly down at the note in her hands. What was he on about? Then she snapped her head up and met his gaze. A sparkle danced in the servant's rheumy eyes. Gratitude filled her breast. "Of course." Her smile widened. "My visit." Imogen allowed the servant to help her into her cloak. She adjusted the clasp at her throat. "How could I forget?"

"You could not," he murmured dryly and hastened to open the door.

With a last thankful look for the faithful butler, she hurried outside, into the cheerfully glaring sunlight. Almost fearing her mother would sense her hasty departure, she bounded down the steps, attracting curious stares from passersby, and made her way to the waiting carriage.

A footman pulled the door open and helped her inside. As the door closed behind her, Imogen settled onto the soft bench. Then, a moment later, the conveyance rocked into motion, she settled into the comfortable squabs of the carriage with a relieved sigh.

It was an inevitability that she would have to confront her sister, and . . . She wrinkled her nose, Rosalind's husband. And where the agony of that treachery had once stuck like knives in her heart, now the hurt was gone, replaced instead with a desire to distance herself from blackhearted people more beautiful than the objects chiseled by great sculptors, yet just as emotionally dead as those same masterpieces.

Filled with a renewed burst of energy, she pulled the curtain aside and peered out at the passing London streets as the carriage rattled along. Since William had broken it off and married her sister, Imogen had become a person she didn't recognize and didn't like. Bitter, melancholy, cynical. It was as though a stranger had taken over her being and controlled her every frown and tart response.

For a long, long time she'd believed herself incapable of smiling. She released the curtain and it fluttered into place. But she had learned to smile again. Alex's tantalizing grin and deliberate teasing barbs slipped into her mind.

From the moment he'd tricked her into gaining permission to call her by her Christian name, he'd opened her eyes to her own brittle aloofness. And she, who'd walked about in a perpetual gloom, was reminded that she'd once loved to smile and laugh.

Imogen groaned and knocked the back of her head against the velvet squabs of her seat. What manner of inherent weakness existed within her that she should be so captivated by a gentleman who'd eye a scandalous beauty across a crowded theater moments after stroking her own palm?

Determined to set thoughts of him from her mind, Imogen gave her focus to the note given her by Masterson. She unfolded the ivory velum.

Do tell me you'll visit. With one brother seeing to marquess business and the other doing scandalous secondson business . . . it is dreadfully horrid with none other than myself for company.

Her lips twitched with amusement and she folded the note. Chloe had long possessed a flare for the dramatics, from their earlier days at Mrs. Belton's Finishing School to their rather weak Come Out together.

Since Rosalind's betrayal, Chloe, in a way, had shown herself to be more of a sister than the woman whose blood Imogen shared. She'd also become a savior of sorts, plucking her from the miserable, uncomfortable wing of her traitorous family and drawing her into the fold of her loving, protective one. And in so doing, thrusting her brother Alex into Imogen's world. As the carriage rattled on, she still could not determine if that was a good thing or an altogether very dangerous occurrence.

The odd rhythm set by her heart, however, spoke to the latter.

Alex lay on the velvet sofa in the library, his jacket from last evening was rolled up into a ball and stuffed under his head, Shakespeare's *Romeo and Juliet* opened and forgotten atop his chest. He swiped a hand over the day's growth of beard on his face and stared up at the nauseatingly cheerful mural painted upon the ceiling, with cherubs locked in an embrace that would have seen most mortals consigned to hell for the scandal of it.

The sky, of pale blues and purples, served as mocking contrast to the dark, vile marquess who'd ordered that work painted, and all the evil deeds he'd perpetuated in here against his own children. Except, staring up at those dancing, plump cherubs atop their bilious, white clouds, the last person he was thinking about was his father.

Imogen, with her satiny-soft skin and flaming-red hair, should elicit nothing more than sinfully erotic thoughts that involved the two of them entwined in one another's arms. But while he ached to bed her and lay claim to her, some great shift had occurred. He who'd before only sought the mindless enjoyment to be had in those meaningless exchanges with scandalous women—craved more. For if this charged awareness was merely sexual in nature, then after he'd left Imogen at the end of the performance, he could have taken one of the beauties at Forbidden Pleasures and drowned out the memory of the flame-haired lady. Instead, he'd returned home, and after torturous musings of Imogen with her generous smiling mouth and shockingly wide eyes, he'd taken up place in the library and hadn't left since.

Only, he'd made the mistake of plucking Shakespeare's damned tale of star-crossed lovers from the bookshelf. If he were being at least truthful with himself, that selection had been no mere coincidence. And he'd read the blasted verse.

O, *that I were a glove upon that hand,*
That I might touch that cheek!

With a groan he rubbed his palms over his tired eyes. "Get hold of yourself, man," he muttered. He was not a man to wax poetic over the hue of a lady's hair or the smile upon her lips. He did not pine and long for ladies. They whispered and set out to entice *him*. Yet, some subtle and terrifying shift had occurred inside him. Something that defied mere carnal interests and drew him to the lady herself. She possessed a quiet resilience and gentle pride he'd not encountered in any of the women to come before her.

A growl rumbled up from his chest and, determined to set aside any desirous musings of Imogen, he drew up his book and covered his eyes with the leather volume. He should seek out his chambers and hopefully then, sleep would come. Alexander made to swing his legs over the side of the sofa when footsteps sounded in the hall.

"Lady Chloe will join you shortly, my lady. She asked that I show you to the library," the butler's voice carried through the wood panel.

He stiffened as a surge of energy ran through him at the identity of the lady even now being admitted.

"Thank you, Joseph," Imogen murmured, and Alex heard the smile in those words.

And the ladies of his acquaintance did not make nice with the servants. This one did. This one was kind and gracious and throwing his whole world into upheaval. The soft tread of her slippers sounded off the walls of the quiet, cavernous space. He really should announce himself. He should stand up and excuse himself. Yes, there were all manner of things he should do.

Then, he'd never been one to do as he ought.

Alex lay motionless, unmoving, as her soft footsteps sounded as she padded about the room. She paused, and he strained, resisting the urge to sit up and see just how the lady occupied herself.

"He quotes Shakespeare," she muttered.

He stilled. Ah, the lady spoke to herself as well. A bothersome affliction he himself had suffered from since he'd been a boy, cowering and afraid of his father, finding reassurance in his own quiet company.

"*He* quotes Shakespeare." The snap of a book being closed filled the quiet. His lips twitched and he suspected the beleaguered "he" she uttered had nothing to do with Primly and everything to do with him. "It could not have been the marquess taken on the role of chaperone," she spoke, her voice just beyond the edge of the sofa, indicating the lady had moved from her previous spot alongside the floor-length shelving.

His amusement immediately faded when presented with a hint of the mercenary quality he'd come to expect in all ladies. From over the rim of the book, he glanced up. Imogen stood, her fingertips resting on the back of the sofa while surveying the room, her gaze flitting about. "If you are searching for Waverly, I'm afraid he's closeted away in his office seeing to important marquess business," he said with forced dryness, hating that he should care she sought out his brother.

Imogen screeched. She slapped her palms against her cheeks, her face wreathed in horror. "How much did you—?"

Alex swung his legs over the side of the sofa and stood. "All of it," he interrupted with no small amount of glee, relishing her discomfiture. He tossed aside the book he'd made little attempt at reading.

Her flushed cheeks deepened further. "You should have announced yourself, sir." Her voice came out strangled, ruining whatever vain attempt she made at ladylike outrage.

Alex wandered around the sofa and she retreated a step. "And miss your very revealing thoughts, my lady?" He lowered his voice to a husky whisper. "Of a gentleman who . . ." He arched an eyebrow. "What was it you said? Quotes Shakespeare?" She made a choked sound and he continued his forward advance. This time, she maintained her position. Fiercely defiant, Imogen jutted her chin out and met his stare. He brushed his knuckles along her jaw. Ah, Lady Imogen Moore, in all her fiery glory, was a sight to behold. "Never tell me it is Primly you desire," he whispered against her cheek.

With her body pressed nearly to his, he detected the faint tremble that shook her frame. "That is not your business." Her eyes, round like moons, took in the thick growth on his cheeks and his state of dishabille. "You're no gentleman, my lord."

A chuckle rumbled up from his chest. "I never professed to be." Alex brushed his lips against the right corner of her mouth. Her audible inhalation sent a breath of mint and honey wafting about, wrapping him in her innocently seductive fold. "I find when we think we're alone, we are our most honest, Imogen." He cupped her neck, running the pad of his thumb over her silken skin. "You'd have my brother, would you?" In spite of that flippant question, his gut tightened at the idea of Gabriel laying claim to her.

Imogen gave her head a shake, as though attempting to loosen whatever pull he had over her. "What are you on about?" She danced out of his reach.

Alexander propped his hip against the edge of the sofa and fixed his gaze on her. "Did you not seek the marquess?"

Her bewildered eyes met his. "What are you talking about?"

He'd not be so tricked by her false protestations. "Oh, come," he jeered. "You revealed your thoughts when you believed yourself to be alone. You wondered as to why you were denied the company of my esteemed brother and saddled with a mere second son."

"Don't be silly." She planted her arms akimbo. "I said no such thing."

Alex shoved himself to his feet. "Did you call me a liar?" he asked on a hard-edged whisper. People had affixed any number of labels to him through the years—rogue, scoundrel, heartless. Not a single one of them would have dared call him—

"I did not call you a liar," she clarified. She dropped her arms to her sides. "I called you silly."

Something else he'd never been accused of. "Madam, I'll not debate the point with you," he gritted out. "I heard you quite clearly."

"Yes, but—"

"And yet, you'd deny it?"

Her color heightened. "Yes, but that is only because you're quite mis—"

"And you've quite expressed your displeasure with my presence on more than one score, Imogen."

"Because I do not want to see you!" Those words exploded from her lips. A vise squeezed about his lungs, making it a struggle to draw in steady breaths. Since that day he'd leaned over the edge of the sofa and found her sitting there staring up at him, Imogen had occupied every corner of his thoughts. In spite of his fascination with her, she remained indifferent to him and not altogether different than any other woman who desired nothing more than the physical pleasure to be experienced in his arms. Why did the truth of that cause this bloody ache in his heart? "I do not want to see you," she repeated those words softly, as though she sought to convince herself. Her gaze skittered away from his and to the door. Did she seek salvation in the appearance of his conveniently absent sister? That rankled all the more.

"You don't wish to see me?" He arched an eyebrow. Determined to not let her know how greatly her dismissal affected him, he closed the space between them, then captured her chin between his thumb and forefinger, forcing her gaze to his. "Tsk, tsk, how very rude of you," he taunted in a bid to protect the walls he'd erected about his heart.

"What would you have me say, Alex?" The muscles of her throat worked spasmodically. "That I'd prefer His Lordship's presence to yours because he doesn't make me wish for, long for, things I've no place longing for?" He released her and stumbled away, panic building once more, but she continued relentlessly. "Would you have me say that with your charm and your blasted quoting of Shakespeare, you make me forget the pledge I took after the Duke of Montrose to never be so imprudent where a roguish man is concerned?"

He flexed his jaw. Annoyance filled every corner of his tightly held being. "You'd compare me to the likes of Montrose?" he tossed, resenting that for the esteem he'd come to place her in, she could relegate him to the ranks of that lecherous, deceptive man who'd betrayed her.

"Come, Alex," she scoffed. "Surely you'll not be a hypocrite." He bristled and opened his mouth to launch a protest. "You stole my moment of solitude quite deliberately, listening while I exposed my private thoughts." Her tone grew increasingly agitated. "And believed I should desire a man for nothing more than his title. Again."

The wounded look in her eyes brought him up short.

Imogen folded her arms under her chest, digging that blade of guilt all the deeper. "You see, Alex, we're more alike than different."

They were nothing alike. She was innocent and unsullied by the true ugliness of the world.

"Oh, aren't we?" she needled, seeming to hear his unspoken words. "You've found me no different than every widow and wedded woman you've ever taken to your bed."

At her words of him with another, his neck heated with shame. He wanted to strike the truth of them from her lips but instead stood there in humbled silence.

"What did they desire of you? A kiss?" Far more than a kiss. "Likely far more than a kiss," she murmured. A fiery curl fell across her brow and his fingers ached with the urge to brush it back. "And as shameful and shocking as it is for me to admit as much, I want your kiss and . . ." Color bloomed on her creamy white cheeks yet again and she drew in an audible breath. "I want more." Imogen dropped her voice. "But it is the more that is different than all those others. Even having been betrayed as I was, I want love, Alexander. I hunger for it, ache for it, and I could never, would never, have the love of a man who makes eyes at any wanton widow."

Her words sucked the thoughts from his mind as he tried to sort through the implications of her admission. Terror built in his chest, pounding madly in the rapid beat of his pulse, drowning out sound.

Imogen's full lips tipped up in a sad rendition of a smile. "You've nothing to say, but why should you? A man such as you would never want my love, my heart . . . and *that* is why I longed for the marquess's presence, because when I am near him, my heart is not endangered."

"I hate this room," he said, and she stilled, eying him through perplexed eyes. "With every fiber of my being, I hate this whole townhouse."

She shook her head in confusion.

And suddenly it was very important in a world where no one truly knew him, in a world where he was desired for his sexual prowess and not much more, that this bold-spirited, beautifully courageous woman know he was more than the blackhearted rogue she'd taken him for. "My father spent years beating the truth of who I am and what I am into me." A dark, empty chuckle escaped him.

Horror lined her face. "Alex," she whispered, and touched trembling fingers to her lips.

Restless, he stepped away from her. He didn't want her pity or her sympathy. He wanted her to understand. "I'm nothing more than the less-desirable second son, whom ladies would take to their beds, not the man who'd truly be desired for anything more." It had been far easier to bury himself in mindless amusements through the years than to be forced to analyze the person he was, the person he wanted to be.

"That isn't true," she said fiercely, fire in her eyes.

"Perhaps," he said simply. "Perhaps not." Alex had spent years being trained to believe one thing and, as a result, couldn't quite separate who he was from who he wasn't. "Regardless, this house, this room, reminds me of all the darkness." He dragged a hand through his mussed hair. "Yet when you are in it, I don't see any of that darkness. You challenge everything I believe of myself and of women." Alex stalked over and took her firmly by the shoulders, angling her close. He ran his gaze over her face. "Until I no longer know who I am or what I am or what I want to be." She threw into question every lesson ingrained into him by his father on Alex's own self-worth. She made him feel worthy, and more, made him want to be a better man—for her.

Her lips parted, emotion bleeding from her eyes. Alex released her suddenly and stepped away. Wordlessly, he retrieved his jacket and, as he walked to the door, slipped the wrinkled black evening coat back on. He paused in the threshold, not looking back. "I was not making eyes at anyone last night, Imogen. Not anyone that wasn't you." This clever, fiercely brave lady had broken through the facade he'd constructed, that of a careless rake, leaving him exposed.

She drew in a soft, shuddery gasp, and too much of a coward to try to make sense of that slight exclamation, he quickly took his leave.

Chapter 8

*I*mogen stared after Alexander's swiftly retreating frame. Her heart in her throat threatened to choke her with the force of her emotion. She touched her hand to her cheek, remembering his words of Shakespeare and now this exposed, raw figure who shared the pain of his past in a bid to explain the bitterness of his present.

Unbidden, her gaze fell upon the forgotten leather volume he'd tossed aside and, drawn to the small book, she picked it up, running her gaze over the title—*Romeo and Juliet*.

I was not making eyes at anyone last night, Imogen. Not anyone that wasn't you.

Imogen sank onto the edge of the seat he'd occupied moments ago? Hours? A lifetime? She stared blankly down at the book in her lap. With one exchange, but a handful of words, Alexander had thrown into question everything she knew or everything she'd thought she'd known of him. The world of black and white had been easier to understand than this now-murky shade of in-between that she didn't know how to make sense of. She'd accused him of hypocrisy, and yet in truth there was no greater hypocrite than herself, for she'd neatly shelved Alexander in a category of unrepentant rogue. She'd never really allowed herself to consider who he'd been before he'd been that man.

Now she knew. And the knowing was so painful. She tightened her hold upon the leather tome in her fingers. He'd shared but one memory of his father and the vile blackness he found in this home, and that memory had opened her eyes to the scarred, broken child he'd been. Tears filled her eyes and she blinked them back. She'd not pity him. She didn't pity him, and yet, several slivers of her heart broke apart and crumpled at thinking of the dark-haired boy he'd been, fearing this room, this home, this—

"Oh, dear, never tell me you're thinking of him again."

Imogen hopped to her feet, the book tumbling from her fingers and falling to the ground with a noisy thump. "Him?" she repeated blankly as her friend sailed into the room.

Chloe rolled her eyes. "You're a dreadful liar," she said, stopping in front of Imogen. "You've not ceased to think of him."

She hadn't. God forgive her, she hadn't. Not since she'd tilted her head back to find Alex staring down at her with the damning piles of scandal sheets littered about her feet. "How did you know?" she whispered. Had she been that transparent to her friend? A panicky sensation built steadily in her chest. Had others at the theater seen her staring up at him longingly?

"You're my friend, silly." Chloe took Imogen's hands in hers and gave a slight squeeze. "I know you loved him."

Loved him? "What?" The question tumbled too quickly from her lips.

Her friend giggled. "Whatever is wrong with you, Imogen? You're all dazed and befuddled."

And at last it made sense. Chloe believed she pined for the duke. "Nothing. I . . . Nothing is the matter," she said at last.

Chloe settled onto the sofa and Imogen allowed her friend to pull her down beside her.

"Why are you so somber?" she asked, all earlier amusement gone from Chloe's intelligent and kindly eyes. "I saw Alex taking his leave down the opposite end of the corridor." Her mouth hardened. "Did he say something to upset you?" By the tension in her tone, Imogen suspected if she said yes, her friend would blister her older brother's ears.

"No," she rushed to assure her. Or rather, in a way it had been his words that had upset her, but not in the ways her friend believed.

"He was angry," Chloe pressed, like a dog with a bone.

Imogen dropped her gaze to her rose-colored satin skirts. "What was he like?" The question slipped out before she could call it back. Her friend looked at her questioningly. "As a child," she asked before her courage deserted her. "What was Ale . . . Lord Alexander like as a child?" This insatiable desire to know more of him made her incautious, needing to know who he'd been back when he'd begun to see his home as a place of darkness.

Chloe released her hands and said nothing for so long Imogen believed she intended to say nothing or had failed to hear the question. A sliver of her wished that her friend mayhap hadn't heard, because how could she explain to this woman, her dearest friend, that Alex had so captivated her?

"He was my protector." Chloe's eyes grew wistful. "My defender." There was something so very sad in her eyes, something not altogether different than what she had seen in Alex's eyes. How odd to know someone so well and yet not at all.

Imogen's voice emerged tremulous and she despised that showing of weakness. "And you needed a protector?" She reached for her friend's hands. They were stiff and cold in her hold, but she held firm, trying to infuse some of her own strength into her dearest friend.

"Don't we all in some way need defending?" Chloe returned, saying nothing and everything all at once. "Our father was a brute," she whispered, her words so barely there that Imogen strained to hear.

A chill snaked down her spine as she recalled Alex's horrifying revelation. Naïvely—nay, foolishly—she'd not allowed herself to believe that such pain had also been visited upon Chloe and her sister. Bile climbed up her throat. Oh God, the fiend had put his hands upon his daughters, even. How had she not known? Why had Chloe not told her? "Oh, Chloe," she said softly.

Chloe drew her hand back and waved it about dismissively. "Alex was so frequently earning our father's displeasure." She glanced about, her wide eyes more fearful than Imogen ever remembered. When she returned them to Imogen once again, she spoke in hushed undertones. "Sometimes I believed he strove to earn our father's displeasure to protect me and Philippa."

Her gaze wandered to a point beyond Chloe's shoulder. How much of Alex's role as rogue had been a carefully crafted ruse, an indolent, second son who'd never earn anything but displeasure from a vile, abusive man? Had he even realized he'd made that transformation to save his sisters?

"Society doesn't know the true Alex," Chloe said, bringing her back to the moment. "They see the carefree rogue and wastrel who finds his pleasures at his club, but . . ." She held Imogen's gaze. "That is not who he is. Nor is it who he's ever been." There was a hard, forceful edge to those words, a steely resolve belonging to an equally protective younger sister.

Unknowing how to respond, Imogen said nothing.

Chloe touched her fingers to her temples and winced.

Concern for her friend replaced her preoccupied thoughts of Alex and Chloe's tragic youth. "Are you all right?"

Her friend gave a wan smile. "Just a bit of a headache."

A wave of guilt flooded her. As long as she'd known Chloe, the young lady had been prone to megrims whenever she was beset by stress or worries. "I'm so sorry," she said, the words wholly inadequate.

"For what?" Chloe asked, far more magnanimously than Imogen deserved. "For caring about my brother, who is my dearest friend?" She flinched again.

"For upsetting you."

Chloe narrowed her eyes as though the thick sunlight penetrating the curtained windows had blinded her and drew in a slow, deep breath. "It is not your fault. You didn't know," she said when Imogen made a sound of protest.

Her guilt redoubled. She should have known. As Chloe's friend and confidante through the years, it should have not taken the words of the woman's older brother to open her eyes to the true hell known by her and her siblings. Just as she should have known there was more to Alex than he presented the world. "You should rest," Imogen murmured, taking to her feet.

Her friend rose slowly. Her stiff, jerky movements hinted at the pain Chloe was in. "I am s—"

"If you dare finish that apology, I shall never forgive you," she warned. Then much the way she'd done when they'd been in finishing school and Chloe was suffering from one of her megrims, she took her gently by the elbow and placed her other arm at her waist and steered her from the room.

"You are a dear," Chloe whispered, her voice faint.

"If I were a dear, I'd not have upset you as I've done," she said dryly, even as concern swirled inside for her friend. The two women fell silent. Imogen had learned long ago that even the slightest sound brought her friend to great pain. She guided her through the corridors, looking about for a servant.

The Marquess of Waverly stepped out of his office and she sent a silent thank you skyward for his timely appearance. He opened his mouth to greet them, but then took in his sister's gray-white pallor and hunched shoulders.

"It is another of her megrims," Imogen said quietly, taking care to not speak too loudly.

The marquess's frown deepened and then in one effortless movement, he swept his sister into his arms. "Lady Imogen," he mouthed, an unspoken thank-you.

Imogen dropped a curtsy as he carried his youngest sister above stairs. As she stood in the silent, empty corridors of these walls Alexander had lived within as a child and grown to abhor, she confronted just how little she knew him and how desperately she wanted to know more.

Chapter 9

*T*he following afternoon, seated in the same library with thoughts of Imogen swirling through his head, Alex stared morosely down into his glass of brandy and then with a curse, took a long sip. His lips pulled in an involuntary grimace as the fine spirits blazed a trail down his throat. He welcomed the sting it left in its wake. The open leather volume stared mockingly up at him.

The lady quoted Shakespeare. And with her calm in facing the vipers of the *ton*, demonstrated a spirit to rival Joan of Arc herself. She detested shopping. Enjoyed reading. And she saw him as little more than one of those indolent, shiftless lords.

Alex swirled the contents of his glass. *Isn't that what you are?*

He'd embraced the role of reprobate he'd stepped so easily into through the years. There were little expectations of one who, as his brother claimed, "whored, gambled, and drank" away his life. Yes, it had been far easier to carry on with those low expectations his father had beat him for as a child and then sneered at him for as an adult. It was a humbling moment for a man of nine and twenty to realize he'd lived a shiftless, meaningless life where his brother's charge held true. Beyond his sisters, no one else mattered.

Except, if that were true, then why in the crowded theater with the recently widowed Viscountess Kendricks staring boldly across at him, an invitation in her eyes, had he been unable to drum up a fledgling of interest? Not one bit of desire had consumed him. There had been—nothing. Only a silent comparison of all the ways in which the viscountess paled alongside Imogen's fiery beauty.

What havoc had Imogen wrought upon him?

Heavy, determined footsteps sounded in the hall. Alex stiffened but maintained his fixed attention on the remaining contents of his drink.

"Never tell me you're drunk at this early hour," his brother called from the doorway.

"Then I won't." Knowing it would infuriate the other man, Alex downed his brandy and reached for the bottle. He filled the glass to the rim. "A pleasure as usual," he drawled, setting the bottle down. "Have you come to task me with further responsibilities? Am I to muck out the stables next?" He reclined in the leather, winged-back chair, cradling his glass between his hands.

With a snort, his brother entered the room and then closed the door behind him. "You'd liken chaperoning your own sister to such a tedious chore, then?"

He remained stonily silent. Instead, he studied the amber droplets clinging to the side of his crystal glass. Four days ago, he'd taken it as the very greatest chore, a punishment doled out by his brother. Now, with the time it had afforded him with Imogen, having spent the days with her—the lady who quoted Shakespeare and boldly met the derision of the *ton*, whose red, bow-shaped lips had haunted his thoughts since their first meeting—his role as chaperone was no chore. No chore at all.

Gabriel wandered over and stopped, his gaze on the open book. "By God, are you reading Shakespeare?"

"Yes. No." He had been, but then Imogen and her naked fingers intertwined with his had driven back thought of all else. His brother eyed him suspiciously but was good enough to let the matter die. Perhaps he wasn't a total bastard after all. When it became apparent that Gabriel intended to stand over him in stoic silence, Alex gritted his teeth. "What do you want?"

Gabriel took the seat opposite him. "I came to speak to you about Chloe."

"Oh?" He quirked an eyebrow.

Then, surprisingly, Gabriel reached for the bottle of brandy and the spare glass on the table between them. He splashed several fingers into the glass. "She is ill."

Alex stiffened and leaned forward in his seat.

Gabriel waved him back. "She has a megrim." His face darkened. "It is a bad one that has lasted the day."

At his brother's words, tension tightened in his belly and Alex was shamed by his own self-absorption for failing to wonder about Chloe's absence. Since she'd been a girl, she'd suffered episodes of debilitating megrims, which he'd often suspected had to do with her own experiences as the daughter of a cruel, brutal lord.

"We did the best we could," his brother said quietly.

Was that supposed to bring some form of absolution? "It wasn't enough." Alex tightened his hold about his glass, the pressure threatening to shatter it. How many years had Chloe and Philippa suffered abuse at the monster's hands?

"It was but a handful of times," Gabriel said, his own guilty gaze fixed on his glass.

"That we know of." Alex managed to grit the words out. The fears he'd carried for so long that he'd been too much of a coward to ask either of his sisters.

Gabriel held his gaze. "It wasn't Mother's fault."

No, it certainly wasn't the diminutive, delicate marchioness's guilt to bear. Though she'd never worn the physical marks speaking to abuse at her husband's hands, neither had she any influence over the late Marquess of Waverly's actions. "I don't blame Mother."

As though he'd been punched in the midsection, the air left Gabriel's lips on a hiss. A spasm of pain ravaged his face. "You were always the better one. You stopped it. When Mother . . ." He paused, his gaze skittering off. "Mother or I failed to end his abuse, you did."

Would his brother make him out to be a hero? For he wasn't. He was flawed and broken and empty. And because he didn't know what to say in response, he said nothing.

Alas, his brother was not content to let the matter rest. "He never forgave you."

Alex forced his lips up into a wry smile. "The way I'd seen it, he hated me anyway." There had been nothing for him, a boy of sixteen, to lose the day he'd taken their sire's birch rod and beat him within an inch of his life for having hit Chloe. She'd been but a child. Pain dug at his insides.

"I should have seen to it," his brother spoke in quiet tones.

"Because you were the heir?" The bond they'd shared, however, hadn't always recognized the distinctions of their birth.

Gabriel met his stare. "Because I was your older brother."

"By a year," he said. Uncomfortable with the emotion he saw in his usually unflappable brother's eyes, he shifted in his seat.

His own regrets were mirrored in his brother's gaze. "And yet, that one year should matter so much." It shouldn't have. Not between two boys who'd grown up as best friends, protectors of one another. Those twelve months had, however mattered a great deal to their father. "I should have beat him bloody for having put that birch rod to Chloe."

"Yes, yes you should have," Alex said unapologetically.

Gabriel cleared his throat and then took a long swallow of his drink. "I didn't come here to fight with you. I came to speak to you about your responsibilities for Chloe."

His brother had surely realized his folly in sending Chloe out into the world with Alex for her chaperone. "Oh?" Knots twisted in his belly at the idea of being removed from those responsibilities—for reasons that had nothing to do with brotherly devotion and everything to do with a flame-haired temptress.

"You are relieved of your responsibilities for the evening."

For the evening.

Some of the tension drained out of him. It was only for the evening.

"I thought you might seem a good deal more enthused about the reprieve, the opportunity to visit your clubs." Those words were spoken matter-of-fact, no recrimination.

"I'm not wholly the self-absorbed bounder you take me for. Have you summoned a doct—?"

"The doctor has already attended her. She will be fine. She requires rest."

When plagued by her megrims, Chloe could not bear even the hint of light. Her curtains were kept closed, her room shrouded in darkness. He clenched his hands, wishing he could beat his father all over again for having touched Chloe and Philippa.

Gabriel finished his drink and set the glass down on the rose-inlaid mahogany table. He stared at the otherwise immaculate surface for a long moment. "For everything you believe, I do not hate you." That was something. "I . . ." He clenched and unclenched his jaw. "There are many things I wish I had done differently when we were younger and for that I'm sorry, but I cannot change the past. The charge I've given you, caring for Chloe, was not a punishment."

"Then what was it?" he tossed back. Gabriel's efforts had borne glaring similarities to their father's attempts at exerting control over those under his influence.

Gabriel glared. "Don't liken me to him. I'm not that man. I'm not him." He placed his palms on his lap and leaned over. "If I were like him, then I'd not care about how you live your life. I'd allow you to become the drunken whoremonger you'd have yourself be."

Alex's insides twisted at his brother's words.

Gabriel shoved to his feet. "Don't become the man he believed you to be. Be the man I always knew you were. Good, honorable, worthy." He opened his mouth as though he wished to say more, and then with a slight dip of his head, took his leave. He closed the door behind him on a soft click.

The muscles of Alex's throat worked and he raised the glass to his lips to toss back the desperately needed burn of the warm brandy. His brother's words echoed around the chambers of his mind. With a curse, he set the glass down so hard on the table before him that liquid splashed over the rim. He swiped a hand over his face not knowing this topsy-turvy world he now existed in. A world in which his brother was not the domineering, commanding stranger he'd been over the years. A world in which a young, innocent lady held more allure than the most experienced siren.

Panic built hard and fast in his chest. Gabriel was wrong. He was the emotionless rogue the world thought him to be. It was no facade. And this, this captivation with the proud Imogen, undaunted by any worthless member of the *ton*, was based on nothing more than lust. He wanted her body. Still craved the taste of her lips. Ached to tug the hem of her gown up, exposing the creamy expanse of her thighs and plunder the fiery thatch at her center.

O, she doth teach the torches to burn bright!
It seems she hangs upon the cheek of night . . .

A groan rumbled up from his chest and he shoved back the futile desires for a lady who required marriage. With the panic flaring once more in his chest, he leaped to his feet.

What's in a name? That which we call a rose
By any other name would smell as sweet . . .

The lady had been right. What a man was mattered. His brother was wrong. There was nothing good, honorable, or worthy about him.

Alex strode from the room, determined to seek out his clubs.

Chapter 10

*P*erched on the window seat overlooking the quiet streets below, Imogen traced a small circle over her palm. Her maid sat quietly in the corner. She expected, as tonight would be the evening of the great reunion between the two Moore sisters at Lord and Lady Ferguson's ball, that she should be filled with some nervous horror about the public display. However, she couldn't drag forth one bit of worry, fear, annoyance, or any emotion between for that meeting.

Alex had thoroughly occupied every corner of her mind since last evening. She studied the intersecting lines he'd teased with the tip of his finger. She'd preferred a world in which she'd consigned him to the ranks of the faithless Duke-of-Montroses of the world; an indolent pleasure seeker who thought nothing of breaking a lady's heart. Because she did not know what to do with this gentleman, the one who presented a hard exterior to the world, while underneath longing to be thought of as more than an emotionless rogue. All she knew was with each day spent in his company he chiseled away at the walls she'd carefully constructed about her heart. With his kiss and his whispered words of Shakespeare making a mockery of those efforts. She'd believed herself in love with William. And yet, since Alex had stepped into her life, she'd not thought of the duke, but with detachedness. Instead, she'd come to eagerly anticipate Alex's teasing, his bold challenges, and . . . his company.

Imogen groaned and beat the back of her head against the wall. "Fool, fool, fool."

Someone cleared their throat at the front of the room and she jerked upright so quickly, she wrenched the muscles of her neck. "Masterson," she said, a heated flush burning her cheeks.

A twinkle glinted in his eyes. "You have a missive, my lady," he said, striding over with the silver platter in hand.

She swung her legs over the edge of the window seat and accepted the small blade and note bearing Chloe's familiar scrawl, enlivened by the indication that her friend was surely faring better since yesterday's megrim. "Thank you," she murmured to the old servant. An excitement stirred in her belly at the prospect of going . . . well, anywhere with her friend's unconventional chaperone. Imogen slid the tip of the knife under the seal, then placed it back upon the tray. "Thank you, Masterson."

"My lady," he said with a final bow and then took his leave.

She turned her attention to the note. Imogen quickly perused the sloppily written contents and her excitement faded. Her friend was indisposed. These bouts of violent headaches Chloe suffered through the years occasionally left her debilitated, unable to move, most times for the course of a day. Sometimes longer. Imogen folded the note and set it aside. Guilt settled in her chest at her earlier self-centeredness in having been focused on Alex and the time she'd be afforded with him.

Another knock sounded at the door.

She glanced up at Masterson. "My lady, you have a caller." Her heart sped up. But for Chloe, there was no one who would call on her and there was just one gentleman she now knew and one gentleman she now wanted to know. "Lord Primly," the butler announced.

It was not this tall, slender gentleman now framed in the doorway. "Oh." The shocked little exclamation escaped her.

His lips turned up in a shy smile. "My lady," he murmured and then offered a deep bow.

Imogen battled back the foolish disappointment that Lord Primly was not, in fact, another. "My lord," she said, sinking into a curtsy. They stood there for a moment, staring awkwardly at one another. From the corner of the room her maid, Lucy, coughed. Imogen warmed and hurried to the red velvet armchair and sat. "Er, yes, would you care to sit?" She motioned to the ivory upholstered sofa opposite her.

"Indeed." Stilted silence followed as he claimed his seat.

Imogen fidgeted with her skirts. "Would you care for tea and refreshments?"

He waved off her offer. "No, no refreshments."

It occurred to her that he wasn't stammering. Odd, it seemed to only occasionally plague the young earl.

A wry smile turned his lips upward. "It is the oddest, most bothersome habit."

She wrinkled her brow. "My lord?"

Lord Primly drummed his fingertips along his blue satin breeches. "My stammering," he said with a directness she appreciated. "I do it when I'm nervous." He leaned over, shrinking the space between them. "And it is the oddest thing, my lady." He passed his kindly blue gaze over her face. Before she could ask for clarification, he said, "I do not stammer when I'm around you. In fact, I find myself quite comfortable with you." Red suffused his cheeks at that bold admission.

And Imogen found his refreshing honesty and shyness endearing. She smiled. "Well, it is likely because you've come to keep company with one of the most scandalous ladies of

Society." At one time, those words would have dripped with bitterness. Now they merely contained an underlying dry amusement.

The young lord shook his head, his expression again somber. "Oh, not at all, my lady." Then he grinned, a dimple marring his right cheek. "I imagine there are any number of more scandalous ladies than you."

A burst of laughter escaped her. Lord Primly scratched his head and it occurred to her that his words had been intended as a compliment more than a jest. She schooled her features and sat back in her seat. Lord Primly clasped his hands in front of him and rubbed his thumbs together in a quick, nervous rhythm, awkwardly silent. She used the moment to study him. Taller than most, the gentleman was rail thin and possessed of a thick crop of luscious golden curls she would have traded her right hand for as a small girl. Not an unhandsome gentleman, and yet, nothing in him roused the sentiments that Alex did with a mere glance from his black lashes.

Lord Primly spoke, interrupting her regretful musings. "I w-would like permission to court you."

Imogen tipped her head, certain she'd heard him wrong, and yet it had sounded as though he'd said—

"If that would be p-pleasing to you, that is."

A woman with her notorious reputation should gladly welcome his very kind, generous offer. "I . . . that would be pleasing to me," she said softly, praying he could not hear the lie to those words.

He beamed.

Why did regret turn inside her heart that it was not another gentleman who'd brave Society's scorn to court her with the most honorable intentions?

Imogen was saved from replying to herself by the sudden appearance of her mother. The countess sailed into the room. She spread her arms wide. "Lord Primly, what an honor."

She cringed at the hint of desperation in that handful of words.

Lord Primly immediately sprang to his feet and bowed deep. "M-my lady."

And yet, for all the discomfort that came with Mother's desperate attempt at matchmaking, there was a good deal of relief at being spared the pained awkwardness in being alone with the young earl.

Mother sailed over in a flurry of silver satin skirts and claimed a seat upon the sofa. "Will you attend Lady Ferguson's ball this evening, my lord? My Imogen will be there."

She winced once more. Perhaps she would be better off without Mother's company, after all.

Lord Primly caught Imogen's eye and gave a slight wink, clearly interpreting her musings. "Then there is no place I would rather be, my lady."

Shock filled her, not at Lord Primly's flowery words but at that bold wink. She'd not taken him as a man who—

Catching her notice of him, he winked again.

They reclaimed their seats and Imogen sat back, content to let Mother fill the void of silence with her ramblings. Some of the earlier tension and reservation fled as she felt the first stirring of gratitude for a gentleman willing to look past her scandalous broken betrothal and court her anyway. It spoke to the man's character and strength. He rose in her estimation.

"I h-have expressed m-my intentions of courting your daughter," Lord Primly said suddenly, unexpectedly.

Mother's eyes lit. "Oh, how very splendid! Splendid, indeed, my lord! My Imogen would make you a splendid cou—"

"Mother," she said sharply, cutting into those humiliating words.

Silence fell once more.

The earl fumbled with his pocket and withdrew a gold watch fob. He consulted the attached timepiece. Then he stood. "I-if you will excuse me. There is b-business I must see to."

Mother appeared crestfallen. "But you've only just arrived, my lord."

Imogen dug her toes into the soles of her slippers with humiliation.

"I-I know. R-regretfully, I must be off." He turned to Imogen and bowed. "M-my lady, I look forward to meeting again tonight." With that, he hastily backed out of the room.

Well, that had not been a gentleman eager to make a match. Her shoulders sank in relief. Likely a result of her mother's shameful, less-than-subtle matchmaking.

Alas, the older woman apparently saw it in a very different light. "How could you be so coolly disinterested, Imogen? With your ill-behavior you've run off the earl," her mother cried.

"I've not run off the earl," she said in a gentle, calming tone. "Lord Primly had matters of business to—"

"This is a disaster, indeed," her mother lamented. She proceeded to pace a hurried path upon the Aubusson carpet. "And you," she paused to jab a finger in Imogen's direction. "You can hardly afford to turn away an honorable suitor such as the Earl of Primly. Not with your scandal."

She gritted her teeth to keep from pointing out that it was, in fact, her sister who'd put her in this position as a gossiped-about, sought-after-by-none young lady on her third Season.

Mother patted the back of her coiffure. "I know your heart was broken." Had it been? At one time, she'd believed that to be the case. "But you must look to your future. Lord Primly, stating his desire to court you, has expressed a very real interest in being part of that future. Do you understand what I'm saying?"

"Yes," she said quietly. Marry where her heart wasn't engaged, to any gentleman who'd have her. And following Alex's unwitting manipulation of her foolish heart, he'd only lent credence to her mother's calls for an honorable, respectable gentleman who would have her. So why, when Lord Primly dangled the possibility of stability and safety with his gentle presence, did she long for more?

Her mother's gently spoken words cut into her musings. "Be gracious to Lord Primly this evening, Imogen."

She stared blankly. "This evening?"

Her mother tossed up her hands. "Lord and Lady Ferguson's," she said, exasperation drawing out those three words.

Oh, God. Lord and Lady Ferguson's. With Chloe ill, Imogen would be forced into this public reunion without the support of her friend, or anyone other than her disloyal kin. Her stomach turned. "I cannot go." She'd convinced herself she was ready to brave the scandal and the gossips. Now she was confronted by her own cowardice. Imogen could not do this, not alone without Chloe by her side. Alex flitted through her thoughts. Or with him. She could brave the devil at dinner with his strong, unapologetic person at her side.

"Do not be silly, Imogen," her mother snapped, her eyebrows forming a single, impatient line. "I've already told you that you must face the gossips eventually."

"I have," she said on a raspy breath. "At the theater and shopping and . . ." And they'd stared and whispered. A ballroom full of those stares and whispers? She could not do that. Not alone. "Tonight is not the night, Mother." Not without the support of a friend. Alex . . .

"Tonight is most certainly the night." Her mother claimed her face between her palms in that infuriating way she had since Imogen had been a girl. "You will feel the better for it. And with Lord Primly favoring you, you too shall wed."

I do not want Lord Primly. Even if he was the safe, comfortable choice in a husband, she longed for another.

Her mother released her and with a pleased nod, sailed from the room.

Short of the Lord smiting Lord Ferguson's townhouse into a fiery inferno, the *ton* would have their Moore sister reunion and Imogen would be as she'd been for so very long—alone.

Chapter 11

*A*lex stared at the bottle of brandy. He should be drunk. He should be, if he'd drunk that damned bottle. Except after spending nearly the entire afternoon and early evening at Forbidden Pleasures, he still nursed his second glass.

His lip pulled back in a disgusted snarl at the fool he'd become. When his friend, Stanhope, had given his heart to the reputedly flighty Lady Anne, he'd mocked the other man for turning over his carefree lifestyle for a respectable miss. After all, what was the intrigue in an unwedded innocent?

Alex took a sip of his drink. It turned out, in knowing Lady Imogen as he now did, there was a good deal of intrigue in those unwedded innocents. Nay, not all of them. One of them. He swiped a disgusted hand over his face.

"Are you looking for company, my lord?" a husky voice purred at his shoulder.

He stiffened and looked up. The barely clad beauty, with hair so pale golden it was nearly a shade of white, fingered her lower lip. Lips that were not full enough nor the shade of crimson berries, and likely a mouth that didn't taste like innocence.

Alex gave a brusque shake of his head and wordlessly returned his attention to his drink. He was going mad. There was no other accounting for the fact that instead of relishing his reprieve from the dreaded role of chaperone, he instead fixed on the tedious passing of minutes, wishing away the day until his sister was able to go out once more with Lady Imogen Moore.

This evening, she would be at Lady Ferguson's ball, where she and her sister and the lackwit Duke of Montrose, would be reunited before the *ton*. He'd spent the better part of the day trying to convince himself it didn't matter if the lady faced the *ton*, weathering the gossips on her own. Tried and failed.

He did care. God help him, he who cared about no one's happiness beyond his own cared about Imogen. His stomach tightened at the idea of her facing the onslaught of the gossips and their vicious whispers alone. He pressed his eyes closed. He should be there. Alex shoved back his chair. He should have been there two hours ago.

"Well, well, Edgerton," a hard, steely cold voice drawled.

He glanced up and bit back a curse. The Marquess of Rutland, one of Society's vilest lords, stood at the edge of his table, a nasty glint in his brown eyes. "Have you been relieved of your responsibilities for the evening?"

Alex snapped erect at the other man's subtle hinting, which made little sense. Rutland wouldn't know any of the private discourse between him and Gabriel. He gave his head a shake. "What the hell do you want, Rutland?" he snapped. Rutland had dueled with his friend Stanhope some years ago. Alex had served as Stanhope's second and that loyal moment had forever cemented the seething hatred Rutland carried for him.

The other man tugged out the chair opposite Alex and, uninvited, claimed a seat. "I've not seen a hint of you at Forbidden Pleasures since you've taken to playing nursemaid." He steepled his fingers and drummed the tips together.

"Chaperone." He'd been playing chaperone. Imogen, in all her fiery glory, danced through his head. And seducer of innocents. He'd also been playing at that.

A mirthless black chuckle rumbled up from the man's throat at Alex's correction.

"In the six hours you've been here, and of the four lovely women to approach you, you've not accepted an invitation from a single one of them. Why is that?" This lethal, probing whisper was likely the same used by Satan when arranging his dark deeds.

Warning bells blared in his mind at the man's studious attention to his actions that day. Ruthless, vicious in all things, there had never been a friendship between them. He forced a lazy, negligent grin. "Bored are you, Rutland? Bored enough to study my goings-on?" Then, he'd wager the garments upon his back that Rutland had never known the friendship of anyone.

"I'm never bored."

No, the calculated bastard had a reputation of toying with the lives of people. One such as him was incapable of weakness and likely had never experienced any emotion. Sorrow. Regret. Pain. Love. He started. Where had that come from? "Why don't you say what it is you've come to say and be gone?" he bit out.

"You've taken to shopping and visiting the theater."

How had the other man gathered where he'd been? He resisted the urge to tug at his cravat. And if he'd gleaned his whereabouts, had he also observed his exchanges with Imogen? The sudden urge to drag the other man across the table and bloody him senseless filled Alex with a tangible force.

"Nothing to say?" Rutland taunted.

Feigning nonchalance, Alex lifted his shoulders in a shrug. "What would you have me say?" With a casualness he didn't feel, he grabbed his glass and took a sip of brandy, not tasting the fine French spirit on his lips. "I know a snake such as you quite enjoys toying with your prey." He swirled the contents of his glass in a deliberate movement. "However, I've never been afraid of you."

Rutland rested his elbows upon the table and leaned forward. "I do not like you, Edgerton."

"You don't like anyone, Rutland," he drawled. "Nor does any member of polite Society bear any good feelings for you." With a grin he tossed back the remainder of his drink.

"You are correct on that score." His hard lips peeled back in a sneer. "However, that is where we two differ. I've never given a jot what anyone thinks of me, and you . . ." He flicked a piece of imagined lint from his immaculate black sleeve. "You've always cared a good deal, haven't you?"

Knowing better than to fall trap to his schemings, Alexander yawned.

Annoyance glinted in the other man's gaze. With a scowl, he eyed the occupants about the club, his gaze lingering a moment upon the fat, lecherous Viscount Waters with a beauty on his lap while he wagered away and lost at the whist tables. The slight narrowing of Rutland's eyes indicated the man had identified prey that would prove far more satisfactory to whatever game he sought to play this night. The calculated marquess returned his attention to Alex, clearly unfinished with him. "So it is the *dear* Lady Imogen—poor, jilted-for-her-sister Imogen—who has bewitched you?"

All efforts at nonchalance lifted and Alex gripped the edge of his table hard enough to leave crescent marks on the smooth, mahogany surface. The desire to bury his fist in the man's smug, mocking face was a tangible life force. "Shut your goddamn mouth." Except those four words merely weakened him in the eyes of this bastard. "She has not bewitched me," he gritted out the belated response. A man such as Rutland knowing how much Imogen mattered to Alex only opened her to a danger she was undeserving of. "She is nothing to me." He lied. In a short time, she'd become everything to him.

A cold, ugly smile turned the other man's lips upward in a macabre grin. "You surprise me, Edgerton."

"Oh?" The history between them should have taught Alex better than to indulge the blackguard's vindictive needling.

Rutland shoved back his chair and stood. "I'd always taken you for one who appreciates the finer beauties." Alex stiffened. "You'd pant after the dull, jilted Lady Imogen . . ." A black curtain of rage descended over Alex's vision, momentarily blinding him. "How unlike you to take some other man's refuse when you can surely have the more beautiful Moore sister in your—"

Fury coursed through his veins and drove him to his feet. He punched Rutland in the face. The other man grunted and stumbled backward, knocking into a table of gaping dandies and then landing in a heap upon the floor. Burning with a seething fury, Alex stalked around the table and towered over Rutland's form. "If you so much as ever mention Lady Imogen Moore's name again, by God I'll see you at dawn this time. You are not fit to speak her name. The lady is more beautiful than any—" He snapped his teeth together so swiftly pain radiated along his jaw. He'd revealed entirely too much before an audience at Forbidden Pleasures. A flurry of loud whispers sounded from those around them.

Rutland shoved to his feet. "How very . . . passionate you are about a woman you profess to have no interest in." He whipped out a white handkerchief from his black jacket pocket and snapped the fabric open. With a triumphant grin, he held it to his bloodied nose.

Nausea churned in his belly. The other man had merely baited him. Of course he cared for Imogen. She was his sister's dearest friend. "There is no interest." *Liar*. His pause too long. The predator too perceptive.

"Of course there isn't." There was a faintly condescending thread to Rutland's tone "Why, a man who takes his pleasure where he would could not give his name to a lady in the market for a husband." He scoffed and, even with the height similarity between them, managed to peer down his aquiline nose at Alex. "What would you, a mere second son who drinks and takes his pleasure with countless whores, have to offer her?"

Those taunting words stuck as well-placed arrows in his chest. His father's cold, mocking tone blended and melded with this vile reprobate's. *Nothing. I have nothing to offer her.* Every ugly accusation flung at him by his father danced to the surface, and yet, God help him, he wanted her anyway. Wanted her in every way. In his bed, in his heart, forever, and then beyond.

A loud humming sounded in his ears and the world dipped and swayed under the enormity of that revelation. He closed his eyes a moment, when he opened them, Rutland's cold smile widened. His tongue, heavy in his mouth, Alex couldn't muster a sufficient reply. Nor was there one. He wanted Lady Imogen Moore, the undaunted, boldly courageous young lady who'd stare down ruthless gossips. He, Alexander Edgerton, the careless, carefree rogue, who, as his brother accused, loved no one more than himself, had fallen hopelessly in love with her.

Rutland's lip peeled back in a victorious sneer and he pressed his advantage. "I expect word to travel rather quickly through town of your gallant defense of Lady Imogen."

Alex registered the gentlemen whispering throughout the hall, fixedly studying their exchange, which stood as testament to Rutland's claim. He staggered back as the ramifications of his admission exposed him before Rutland and the rabidly curious noblemen present and worse—himself. He felt splayed open, bared before all. He struggled to set to order his riotous emotions. Unsuccessfully. He was drowning and couldn't find air.

"Though I daresay," Rutland said, calling his attention back. "You'll merely earn pity for having come to care for a lady," he jeered. "After all, what lady would wed you, the spare, when she aspired to a duke, and even now has earned the attention of an earl?"

Primly. His mind went blank. "Go to hell," he managed, his voice coming out garbled.

Rutland flicked another imaginary piece of lint from his sleeve, so flippant when Alexander's world had been flipped. "I've been there for some years now." The relish in his tone indicated he was quite comfortable keeping company with the devil. Rutland looked up and pierced him with a hard stare. "You see, I long ago vowed to not be shamed at the hands of anyone. Inevitably, I always have my revenge, Edgerton." With a jerk of his chin, he said, "And the day you aligned yourself with Stanhope on that dueling field, you earned yourself a powerful enemy." He swept a bow and then motioned to the front of the club. "I imagine you have somewhere to be?"

Imogen. Montrose. Her sister. His heart raced. He should have left earlier, instead of indulging this madman. Alex turned to leave.

"Oh, and Edgerton." He froze and craned his neck back to look at Rutland. "I had the opportunity to take in a production two nights ago." Rutland grinned that cold, empty smile. "Fascinating play, *Romeo and Juliet*. I did rather enjoy the performance."

Alex spun on his heel and strode from his club.

Christ.

Odd how one could be at the center of a sea of twirling dancers and laughing lords and ladies and yet still be so very alone.

Imogen stood beside the wide column. Near the front of the ballroom, she chatted with Lady Ferguson. The women had been prattling on for the better part of an hour, which Imogen quite suspected had more to do with the hostess hoping to be close when the Duke and Duchess of Montrose entered her hallowed ballroom than in any real *friendship* for Imogen's mother, the Countess of Grisham. Imogen sighed. Since Chloe's note had arrived that afternoon, she'd spent the better part of the day dreading this inevitable meeting and the attention surrounding it. Now she wished her dratted sister and brother-in-law would arrive so they could be done with the exchange and move on.

From behind her shoulder, a flurry of whispers cut into her musings followed by overly loud giggles. Imogen gritted her teeth, having tired of the amusement being had at her expense. The poor, pitiable Moore sister.

". . . Chose the far prettier sister, he did . . ."

Imogen winced as the deliberately loud whisper carried to her ears, hating that she was alone, desperately longing for someone to stand shoulder-to-shoulder beside her. Not in the detached way her mother had for the better part of the evening, but with someone who'd boldly face down the gossips and dare them with his eyes to dare speak a foul word . . .

His eyes . . .

Imogen pressed her eyes closed. And why did this nameless someone possess jade-green eyes and a seductive smile? When she opened hers once more, Lord Primly stood before her. He gave her a wide, unfettered, and *unseductive* smile. "Lady Imogen."

But he was there when no other gentleman had dared brave the scandal of asking the Duke of Montrose's jilted bride for so much as a dance. She smiled back. "Lord Primly, it is a pleasure to see you." And it was. For the first time this evening, she was not alone.

"As we'd been introduced, I did not believe it forward that I've approached you for a dance." He coughed nervously. Alex would send the rules of propriety to the devil. "May I claim one of your waltzes, my lady?" She hated that she mentally compared the two gentlemen.

Imogen stared dumbly up the length of his tall, lanky frame, blinking wildly. "Dance?" No gentleman had so much as wanted to share the same air with her, let alone dance. Her mother paused midconversation with Lady Langley and nudged her none too gently in the side. "Yes. Of course," she said hurriedly.

He scanned her otherwise empty dance card and scratched his name down. "I look forward to it, my lady." With another smile, he dipped a bow, and then strode away.

Imogen glanced down. He'd claimed a waltz. She blinked again. Nay. He'd claimed two waltzes.

A commotion stirred at the front of the hall. The flurry of whispers like a thousand buzzing bees freed from their hive. A pit formed in her stomach as she braced for the soon-to-be meeting with her sister, which would unleash the next wave of malicious gossip. She squared her shoulders and looked to the front of the room.

At Alex.

She blinked once. Twice. And then a third time. What was he doing here? Lord Alex Edgerton most certainly did not attend polite Society functions. That was, not unless there was some lovely widow whose bed he sought. *The Viscountess Kendricks*. Of course. Imogen recalled the lush beauty's sultry invitation to the *seductive* young lord across the theater. Imogen's heart plummeted somewhere to her toes.

Impossibly elegant in his black evening attire and stark white cravat, Alex towered over most of the guests, commanding the room's attention. His intent green gaze scanned the crowd, searching, hunting.

Pain twisted in her belly. It didn't matter that he sought out another. It didn't. *It didn't*. Perhaps if she repeated the litany in her mind, she might believe it.

Imogen dropped her gaze to the card tied about her wrist, taking in the gentleman's name there, a reminder of the safety and security she would know in wedding a man such as the Earl of Primly. She suspected the gentle, oft-smiling Lord Primly would be a steadfast companion—even if he never aroused any of the grand passion she knew for Alex.

Her skin pricked with the sting of awareness and she picked up her head. From across the sea of twirling waltzers, her gaze collided with Alexander's. The green irises of his eyes, hot, penetrating, fixed on her. Then a slow, seductive grin tipped his lips up at the corner. Her heart fluttered and she searched for the recipient of that tempting smile. When she looked across the floor once more, he'd disappeared. Imogen ran her quick stare over the ballroom. Where had he . . . ?

"Are you searching for someone, my lady?"

She slapped a hand to her breast and faced him, hating the way her weak heart quickened. "You startled me."

Alex stood, a glass of champagne dangled effortlessly in one hand, the ghost of a smile on his lips indicated he knew very well whom she'd been searching for. He downed the contents in one long, slow swallow.

Imogen narrowed her eyes as some of her desire lifted. The arrogance of him. "In fact, I was searching for some-one," she murmured.

He tensed as all hint of teasing fled, leaving his face in a cool, hard mask. "Oh? And who is the illustrious gentleman to have captured your notice, sweet Imogen?"

She wet her lips and instinctively drew her dance card close to her person.

His dark eyes followed that nearly imperceptible move-ment. He placed his empty glass upon the tray of a passing servant and reached for her wrist.

Imogen drew it back. "What . . . ?"

Effortlessly, he wrapped his long fingers about her deli-cate wrist and studied her nearly empty card. "Primly," he said, his voice curiously blank. He relinquished the card. "Primly," he repeated.

"Er . . . uh yes," she lied.

He dropped his voice to a low, hushed whisper that wrapped around her. "You were not looking for Primly, Imo-gen. A man such as Primly would be burned by a woman of your fire and passion."

Warmth unfurled in her belly. No one had ever seen her as anything but demure, the always-proper, elder, less lovely Moore sister. He made her feel so much more than that and yet, he would do so at the expense of poor Lord Primly. "You

would disparage the earl? He has been kind and respectful."
And he didn't seem to give a jot about the scandal surrounding her and Rosalind.

"You long for more than kind and respectful," he said, his
words reaching dangerously inside with an unerring accu-
racy. "You want to know passion and desire."

And love. I want to know love. "You're wrong. There is something to be said for kindness and respectability." A muscle
jumped at his eye. Did he take her words as an admonition?

"Kindness and respectability would grow tedious for one
such as you."

"They wouldn't." She tipped up her chin. "And you know
me so well, Alex?" She dropped her voice to a hushed whisper, and there on the fringe of Society said, "If you truly knew
me, you'd know that I crave those sentiments above all else."

"Even after Montrose?" he asked bluntly.

Especially after Montrose. Imogen gave a terse nod. That
bounder's defection had only proven she deserved more,
wanted more—to be loved and respected and honored. And
she wanted Alex to be the gentleman she knew him to be so
he might fulfill all those greatest wishes she carried in her
heart.

Alex claimed her wrist once more. "I know you enough
to see that you long for more and that you would never be
happy in an empty marriage to one such as Primly."

"And who would I be happy in a marriage to, Alex?" She
bit her cheek, wishing to call the words back.

Alexander stiffened, the pencil at her wrist frozen in his
fingers. He raised his eyes from the card a moment to hold
her stare. "Not Primly," he said, at last. Her skin burned in
an ever-awareness of him. He dashed his name upon the card
and straightened.

Imogen didn't know how to account for the inexplicable disappointment coursing through her. *Did you expect his answer should have been him, silly ninny?*

The orchestra concluded the lively country reel and the dancers came to a stop, politely clapping and taking their leave of the dance floor. The faint, haunting strands of a waltz filled the ballroom. "Dance with me." He held out his arm.

She placed her fingertips upon his sleeve and allowed him to escort her upon the dance floor. He settled his hand upon her waist and guided her palm up to his shoulder. "Why are you here?" *Let his answer be for me.*

He flexed his jaw. "Because I wanted to be." His answer was commanding and unrepentant.

"That isn't an answer," she pressed. "Until this Season, I've only seen you at a handful of polite events."

Alex grinned. "Have you been watching for me, love?"

In the time she'd come to know him, she'd recognized his flippantness was nothing more than a protective measure he adopted to discourage intimacy. "No," she said quietly. "I've not been watching you." The truth was that a secret, forbidden sliver of her soul had been intrigued by her friend's bold, unrepentant brother. "Do not try to distract me."

He stared at her through thick, dark lashes, all earlier levity gone. "I came for you."

She stumbled, as he at last delivered those words she longed for. "Wh—?"

With sure movements, he easily righted her. "I came for you."

Then on the heel of that revelation was the stunning, staggering truth. "You didn't want me to be alone this evening."

His mouth tightened, a dull flush staining his cheeks.

Imogen widened her eyes. "Are you blushing?"

Alex mumbled a curse under his breath that would have burned the ears of most proper ladies. "I most certainly do not blush," he said with such haughty arrogance she snorted.

"You are now." She discreetly motioned to his face. "Your cheeks, all the way down to your—"

"For the love of Christ, Imogen, put your hand on my shoulder."

She hurriedly complied. They waltzed on in silence. Smiling up at him, Imogen broke the silence. "I'm sorry I made light of you. Thank you for giving me your support." Up until this moment, but for Primly, she was to be alone to face the vipers of Society this evening.

"Do not thank me," he bit out.

"You have been a friend to me here when—"

His hand tightened once more about her waist. "Is that what you believe?" She winced at the pressure of his touch, and he lightened his hold. "That I am here because of a friendship between us?" When said in that husky whisper she conceded the foolishness in believing any level of friendship could exist between the two. Not when her every sense stirred from his presence alone. "There is nothing the least bit friendly in my being here, Imogen. I am here because I desire you," he said with a boldness intended to shock.

Imogen lightly squeezed his forearm. "I don't believe that is the only reason you're here." She expected a protest from him.

A flurry of interest at the front of the ballroom cut into whatever words were on his lips. She looked disinterestedly toward the entrance of the room. Alexander caught her as she stumbled.

Her sister, Rosalind, stood framed at the entrance in a shimmering, gold satin gown. The chandeliers cast her in an almost haunting glow. At her side stood the Duke of Montrose. They presented a stunning picture of English perfection; he a golden Adonis, Rosalind a delicate, blonde beauty, and everything Imogen with her flaming-red tresses had never been.

Imogen braced for the familiar feelings of longing, regret, the gripping agony of William's betrayal. Instead, on Alexander's arm, for the first time, she acknowledged how wholly inadequate the other man was; in looks, in temperament, and his own worth. Odd that polite Society should so revere the one gentleman for being a duke, permitting unpardonable behaviors, while Alex should prove constant at her side, in spite of the reputation he'd established for himself.

Alex's flinty stare upon her called her attention back to him and away from the horrifyingly fascinated lords and ladies gaping from her to her recently wedded sister. She smiled. "Thank you," she mouthed.

He gave her a slow, gentle smile, devoid of all the cold, harsh cynicism she'd come to expect of him.

Oh God. If he could keep it safe, her heart would be forever his.

Under the rapidly building terror flooding her being, the music drew to a stop. Alex, so coolly unaffected by her presence, guided her to the column. And instead of turning on his heel, he fixed himself at her side.

And she knew her heart would forever be his regardless of how safe he'd keep it.

Chapter 12

*A*lex had no place being beside Imogen in this intimate, if public, reunion between a fractured family. The Lord Alex Edgerton he'd been when first presented with that blasted order of chaperonage or a lack of funds would have ran as far away and as fast as possible from the young lady at his side. Hell, he'd not have sought her out in the first place. No, he'd have been firmly, comfortably ensconced at Forbidden Pleasures.

Yet, everything had changed. In a few short days. Because of her, and more, because of his love for her.

Imogen's mother, the dowager Countess of Grisham, rushed over with a smile on her face. "Im—" She blinked in an owl-like manner at the position Alex had set for himself as sentry, then gave a distracted smile. "Lord Alexander, I trust your brother is well."

Greed flashed in the woman's eyes. *What would you, a mere second son who drinks and takes his pleasure with countless whores, have to offer her?* Rutland's words still burned. Of course the countess would have a marquess for her daughter. Then any titled gentleman would certainly do before a mere second son. "My entire family is well, my lady. The marquess is . . . very . . . marquess-like." From the corner of his eyes, Imogen's lips twitched with amusement.

The countess wrinkled her nose in confusion and then gave a pleased smile. "Just splendid. Do tell him I was, of course, asking after him." She dropped her voice to a conspiratorial whisper. "I quite believe my Imogen would make a splendid marchi—"

"Mother," Imogen snapped.

The older woman gave her head a shake. "Oh, yes, yes. Of course." She took Imogen by the hand. "Your sister and her husband are here, Imogen!" She swept her hand wide, gesturing toward the sea of faces now staring back at them.

The crowd parted to allow the Duke and Duchess of Montrose to continue their forward path to Imogen.

An unholy rage settled in Alex's gut and filled him at the countess's total lack of regard for Imogen. Imogen caught his eye over her mother's shoulder and gave him a soft smile. He shook his head. He'd never before known a woman more courageous. How easily she stared down the face of this unkind scrutiny. He wanted to slip his hand into hers and give her his strength, but he didn't have that right. So instead, he stepped back, wishing he was entitled to that place beside her. Imogen deserved more. She deserved the respectability and goodness she sought . . . and so much more.

The duke and duchess came to a stop before them. Imogen's sister peered down a pert nose at her sister. "Hullo, Im." A victorious smile wreathed her cheeks.

Imogen's face remained carefully expressionless. "Rosalind," she returned, stiffly polite. Then she added, as if an afterthought. "Your Grace," she dipped a quick, and by Alex's thinking, insolent curtsy. Pride swelled in his chest. Ah, God she was brilliant.

The Duke of Montrose's hard gaze lingered a long moment on Imogen. Something primal and possessive roared to life in Alex's chest at the glint of interest he detected in the man's improper stare. "Imogen, I—" The duchess cast a fiery glance up at him. He coughed into his hand. "We have missed you," he corrected.

"Have you?" Imogen drawled, her tone as dry as autumn leaves. Her mother nudged her in the side with her elbow. "Oomph. That is, I'm sure you have."

The countess's nervous laughter trilled loudly, as those around them strained to hear the source of that tense mirth.

Interest lit Montrose's eyes and, because a rogue could detect a fellow rogue from across the English Channel, Alex realized—the man still wanted her. Another surge of possessiveness flared to life in Alex's chest as he was besieged by the unholy desire to tear apart the other man limb by limb.

The duchess wisely wrapped her fingers about her husband's coat sleeve. "If you will excuse me. Im, it is so lovely seeing you. It is unnatural for sisters to not be friendly." Montrose gave a faint shrug, dislodging her touch. His wife blushed a furious shade of red.

"Indeed it is," the countess concurred, clasping the duchess's hand and giving it a squeeze. Mother and daughter stood, smiling at one another. Imogen, however, eyed the two women as though they now acted out the lines of an unfamiliar play. And just like that, the much anticipated reunion was at an end. The lords and ladies present released an anticlimactic sigh and then the event resumed as it had. "Oh, it is so wonderful to have my children together once again," the countess beamed.

Alex curled his hands into tight fists at his side. Montrose shot a glance over his shoulder and his gaze collided with Alex's. The duke narrowed his eyes, casting a possessive look in Imogen's direction. Alex stilled. By God, Montrose didn't want him near Imogen. He didn't want anyone near her. The filthy letch wanted his sister-in-law for himself.

A familiar stammer cut into that scandalous revelation. "H-hullo, my lady." Lord Primly shuffled back and forth upon his feet, a blush on his pale cheeks. "I-I had hoped t-to claim my set."

What lady would wed you, the spare when she aspired to a duke, and even now has earned the attention of an earl . . . ?

Imogen hesitated a moment. "Good evening, Lord Primly." She placed her fingertips upon the other man's sleeve and allowed him to lead her upon the dance floor. For a waltz.

Primly had claimed a waltz. *Of course he had*, a voice jeered. The young earl was deliberately, yet politely, declaring his interest in the lady. Alex gritted his teeth so hard pain radiated up his jaw. It couldn't have been a proper country reel or a quadrille but instead a dance in which his blasted fingers were upon Imogen's slender waist and—

"Please send my regards to your sister, Lord Alex," the dowager Countess of Grisham said politely. "Imogen indicated Lady Chloe was indisposed."

Alex stiffened at the older woman's interruption. "I will be sure to pass along your regards, my lady." He sketched a bow. "If you'll excuse me?" Without awaiting a response, he strode along the perimeter of the ballroom with his gaze trained on Imogen as the ever-proper, blushing Primly guided her awkwardly about the dance floor. The young earl stomped all over her feet. Most young ladies would be frowning, scowling misses. Imogen merely smiled up at the man, eliciting one of those love-struck gleams from Primly's dim eyes.

She'd make the bumbling lackwit a perfectly flawless English wife. Her smile would restore the man's confidence in himself and together they'd become any other married lord and lady hosting their blasted balls and someday presenting their own damned daughters before polite Society and . . .

Alex took a long swallow of his champagne. By God, he needed something a good deal stronger than the light, bubbling champagne. He needed the sharp burn of God-awful whiskey, and more, he needed to get well and truly soused because then mayhap the pain of watching another court her wouldn't be so great.

There really was no purpose in him remaining. He'd put in an obligatory appearance, offering the lady a show of support. He should return to his club and take any number of the four beauties who'd approached him earlier at Forbidden Pleasures. Rutland's baiting had merely opened his eyes to the truth—he loved Imogen. She was better off with another and he should let it all go hang—Montrose's unnatural interest in his sister-in-law, the fawning Primly, and the wistful Imogen.

A figure sidled up to him. "Lord Alexander," the Viscountess Kendricks purred her greeting.

He stiffened, momentarily shifting his attention from the siren upon the dance floor to the notorious widow. "My lady," he drawled. He passed an eye over the woman's dampened gold-satin gown.

She trailed the tip of her tongue along the seam of her rouged red lips, noting his study. "Not your usual entertainment, is it, Lord Alexander?" Her question roused a reminder of Rutland's earlier charge and his own volatile reaction to the man's deliberate jab. The lush widow stroked her fingers along her plunging décolletage. "I find myself bored as well." He'd never said he was bored. In fact, he'd been anything but since the moment he'd stepped in the hall and found Imogen with his eyes. Lady Kendricks dropped her voice to a husky whisper. "I daresay we might enjoy ourselves a good deal more in Lord Ferguson's library."

His thoughts remained fixed on another woman with flaming-red tresses kissed by shades of a summer sunset. *You enjoy reading, do you, Imogen?* "Do you read, my lady?" *Yes I do. Does that surprise you . . .*

The widow's sapphire-blue eyes widened in her face and then she threw her head back on a full, sultry laugh. "Oh, you've the most wicked humor, Lord Alex."

The viscountess angled her body closer to his. Her breasts crushed the sleeve of his jacket. "You and I know there are far better delights to be found in a library, don't we?"

At any other moment, he'd have allowed the blousy figure to follow him from the ballroom then take her hard and fast inside one of his host's rooms. *Go. Take her. Be the man you truly are. Not that false one Imogen and Gabriel believe you to be.*

"My lord?" she whispered once more, a victorious glint in her cynical eyes.

He could not. For even if he followed the viscountess, there would be no surcease. Alex would still hunger for another and crave that which he had no right to. Unbidden with this gaze, he sought the siren who'd so ensnared him.

What have you done to me, Imogen?

Alex studied her over the rim of his champagne flute, as he had for the better part of the evening. At the heated intensity of his eyes, warmth unfurled in Imogen's belly. She forcibly dragged her gaze away and returned it to the polite, proper gentleman who'd been kind enough to court her when no others had.

"You seem distracted, my lady," Lord Primly observed.

Imogen winced as Lord Primly stomped on her toes once more. She mustered a smile. Her poor toes were likely never to recover. "Do I? Forgive me." She'd never been one of those loquacious ladies capable of clever discourse. Likely why her betrothed had jilted her for her sister. She sighed. "I fear my mind is elsewhere," she conceded.

"Upon your sister and the Duke of Montrose, I imagine."

Imogen lost her footing and, this time, Lord Primly righted her. And when faced with no proper response, she said nothing.

"May I say, you handled yourself splendidly. I daresay I would never handle myself with such aplomb," he murmured.

She smiled gently up at him. "I daresay your willingness to defy Society's scorn by courting me speaks volumes of just how you handle yourself in all matters, my lord."

His cheeks reddened under her sincere praise. He glanced about, that slight move caused him to lose his step once more. "May I speak candidly?"

She thought him too much of a proper gentleman to do anything of the sort. "Of course."

"Since our first meeting I've thought of you and all our exchanges often, my lady."

Her mind raced. They'd but spoken on two . . . three, occasions?

As though following the unspoken direction of her thoughts, he said, "Four." She furrowed her brow. "We met at North Bond Street, in your parlor, the theater, and now here."

Oh, sweet Primly. He possessed a gentle spirit and romantic heart. So why could he not be enough? Because the heart knew what the heart wanted. It could not be controlled or dictated or coaxed with logic or reason.

At her silence, he continued. "I would like you to think on . . ." His cheeks reddened and he cleared his throat. "I would like to visit you tomorrow. I ask you to consider whether you'd be amenable to my suit." He hesitated and then rushed ahead. "I would also say that marriages are made every day on a good deal less than what we share."

On a good deal less than what? She tamped down the question, instead focusing on the implications of that request. "I do not truly know you, my lord." Not in the way she now knew Alex.

"I enjoy sugar biscuits and cold ham. I despise brandy." Well, that was certainly in the gentleman's favor. He cleared his throat. "Lady Imogen, I am comfortable around you and I believe you are comfortable around me. There is something to be said for comfort." Yes there was. And immediately following the Duke of Montrose's betrayal, she believed she craved a comfortable, respectful match more than anything else. Now she wanted far more than comfort—she desired the tumultuous sentiments of love and passion and desire.

Unwittingly, she sought out a gentleman who unrepentantly drank brandy in the presence of ladies. She tripped over Lord Primly's feet. A dull humming sounded in her ears. Imogen managed a jerky nod, unable to remove her gaze from the scandalous tableau of the dark-haired, voluptuous Lady Kendricks pressed against the dark-as-sin Alex.

"Are you all right, Lady Imogen?" Lord Primly asked, his voice coming as if down a long hall.

She recalled their exchange just yesterday afternoon in the marquess's library, knew this showing with the sultry widow was just that, a show, a facade he presented to Society. To her. And yet . . .

Her heart cracked and bled, there on the dance floor for all to see.

"And I would be a faithful husband to you." Lord Primly displayed a remarkable astuteness for one who believed marriages were made on biscuits and ham.

The music drew to a stop. "I . . ." Her mind spun, trying to piece together the words he'd put to her. Ham. Biscuits. Brandy. Marriage. "I will consider your offer." He escorted her from the dance floor.

Imogen sought support from the column and detested herself for caring for Alexander as she did, for how she would shamefully search for him, even still. She'd imagined there could be no greater pain than William's betrayal. In this moment, she appreciated how naïvely wrong she'd been.

This was worse. She hated that, even in his pretense as a rogue, Alex should so devastate her with that empty display with the tempting Lady Kendricks. Dratted tears blurred her vision and before she made a cake of herself before all of Society, she hurried along the perimeter of the ballroom. She slipped from the room and all but sprinted down the long darkened corridor, racing anywhere—as long as it was away. With a ragged gasp, she shoved open the nearest door and stumbled into Lord Ferguson's office. She quietly closed the door behind her. A sob tore from her throat.

"Imogen?"

Her eyes flew open. "Alex?" she croaked and then with a dawning horror, the implications of his presence registered. Oh, God. She cast a frantic glance about the room and a giddiness filled her at the confirmation of her earlier supposition. He'd not come to meet the Viscountess Kendricks.

He strode over. "Are you searching for someone?"

"Yes. No. Yes." A useless tear slid down her cheek.

"Montrose?" That one word utterance, a name that came out on a lethal whisper.

Imogen whipped around, and then it occurred to her . . . "You think I'm here to meet the duke?" His silence stood as confirmation. Did he continue to believe so little of her that he consigned her to the ranks of the Viscountess Kendricksses of the world? Another tear streaked down her cheek. "I am most certainly not here to meet the duke. And not merely because he is my sister's husband but because I have more honor than that." She swiped at the bothersome tear. Her sister had stolen her betrothed, but Imogen was incapable of treachery where Rosalind, or anyone, was concerned.

Alex wiped a teardrop with his thumb, the concern in his warm gaze nearly unbearable. She could not properly hate him when he was this gentle, tender stranger. He made a tsking sound. "The woman I've come to know who boldly faces down the gossips with her head held high would not be hiding."

At his opinion of her, warmth unfurled in her heart and she, for the span of a moment, forgot he now sought out another because he was here. "At one time I would have been hiding." She laid a hand upon his and locked their fingers together, studying them entwined. "I marvel at the scared, cowering, young girl I once was." Imogen stole a glance upwards. "I'm no longer that girl, Alex. I'm a woman who's known betrayal and heartbreak."

"And life changes us, doesn't it?" His expression grew dark. "The people we once were change into figures we no longer recognize."

Those words admitted her deeper into his past. "Oh, Alex. What did he do to you?" She ached to know everything there was to know of the man he'd been and what had happened to turn him into the man he'd become.

A vein pulsed at the edge of his temple. Of course, the notoriously hardened rogue would not welcome such an intimate probe from a young lady. "My father was a monster." For a long moment, she believed she'd merely imagined that quiet utterance. His face set in an unreadable mask,

Alexander retreated a step. She longed to call him back, but instead of leaving, he strode to the window in the corner of Lord Ferguson's office.

Imogen took a step toward him, then another, her feet carrying her to his side. She stopped just beyond his shoulder and hovered hesitantly. His silence should serve as all the evidence needed that he had little desire to partake in this particular discussion.

"I've no place telling you what a vile, abusive bastard he was."

His words shot through her, jerking her erect. Except, since his brief admission in the Marquess of Waverly's library, she'd needed to hear the rest from him and she suspected he needed to tell it just as much. Imogen closed the few steps distance between them, and stood at his side, so close their arms brushed, knowing her silence was somehow needed more than anything else in this moment, knowing intuitively that Alex had never before shared the agony of his past and did so now of necessity—to finally be free of his own demons.

He peeled the curtain back and stared out into the darkened street. "A proper marquess that did something as plebeian as beat his children." Alex shot a half-grin down at her. That chillingly empty smile wrenched her heart. "One would hardly ever expect it of the distinguished lord." Those words were steeped in bitterness. "He delighted in reminding me what a failure I was early on." A chuckle rumbled from his chest. "The birch rod was his favorite mode of punishment." Nausea churned in her belly at what he'd endured. "The marks intended to serve as a reminder of those failings. To make me stronger," he spat.

Imogen folded her arms about her waist and hugged tight. "Oh, Alexander," she whispered. Agony lanced through her heart. "I am so—?"

He arched an eyebrow. "Sorry?"

Yes, she was. Sorry for the pain he'd suffered as a boy, pain that had shaped him into a cynical, detached lord who avoided emotional entanglements and took his pleasure where he would.

"I assure you, I do not want pity from *you*."

Imogen tipped her chin up, unfazed by the patently false sneer on his lips. She too had once sought to protect herself at all costs. "I wouldn't pity you, Alex. I marvel that you were strong enough to become the gentleman who—"

"Who what? Became a profligate gambler?" He spoke harshly, merciless in his demands. "A drinker? A whoremonger?"

Imogen recoiled, and then drew in a breath, knowing he merely intended to shock. "You're not really that man," she said, recognizing that with certainty. Mayhap, in some part deep inside, she always had. "You can present the image of indolent rogue to the *ton* but you're not one of those men, Alex." In truth, he had far more honor and courage than any of the peers she'd known in her twenty, almost twenty-one years. She thought of his devotion to Chloe, remembered her friend's words. "You are a dedicated brother—"

"Who didn't even want to be tasked with the responsibility of chaperoning my own sister?"

"And you are here," she said softly. "You came here tonight so I wouldn't face my sister and the duke alone." By the slight pause, she knew her supposition had been correct. Imogen took a step away from him. "I'm sorry I interrupted your tryst."

"Is that what you believe?" Alex jerked his angry gaze toward her. "That I'm here to meet—?"

"The Viscountess Kendricks?" She raised an eyebrow. "Aren't you?" She'd not doubted his interest in the woman was feigned. "What are you doing here, Alexander?" she asked quietly.

"I already told you, I—"

"Not here, but at Lady Ferguson's." Imogen waved her hand about. "You claim you're not here for an assignation. So then why—?"

"You'd have faced your sister and Montrose on your own." The words burst from him. He blanched as her suspicions exploded into truth.

Warmth suffused her heart and nearly set the organ ablaze. He cared. "And that is why your father was wrong and why you aren't like the Duke of Montrose and why you aren't the heartless rogue you've presented to Society." She braced for his protest.

Instead, his shoulders sagged slightly. The muscles of his throat moved up and down. "You'd make me something I'm not," he said in wooden tones.

Imogen returned to his side. "No, Alexander." She cupped his face in her palms, running the pads of her thumbs over his hard, chiseled cheeks. "I'd have you be the man you truly are. Oh, Alex, you still don't realize, do you?" Her heart ached. "Just because one is born a nobleman doesn't mean they possess more honor and integrity than . . ." A second son. ". . . anyone else, does it?"

His jaw worked. "No, that is true."

Polite Society revered lords and ladies for their rank above all else, often turning a blind eye to the dark truths and sins carried by those *illustrious* peers. She touched his forearm. "You agree with me, but why do I suspect you don't truly believe those words?"

At her murmured response, his body went taut, the muscles straining the confines of his black coat. His eyes darkened. "What if I said I came tonight because I want you," he said on a husky whisper that ran through her. Did he intend to shock her? From the moment she'd picked her gaze up and found him grinning down at her in the Marquess of Waverly's library, he'd robbed her of the ability to be scandalized by his actions or words. He roped his arm about her waist and drew her close.

Her belly fluttered, but she tamped down her body's natural yearning for him. "Do you know what I believe?" She didn't wait for him to reply. "I believe your life is no different than one of those Drury Lane productions we took in two evenings ago." He blanched. "You are not a rogue." She'd come to that realization in the theater and now his presence at her side this evening proved him to be more than that feckless fellow. "'In thy face I see the map of honor, truth and loyalty.'"

He started and then adopted that false, rogue's grin—a practiced, deliberate smile. A show. "I most certainly am, my lady." Alex cupped the back of her neck angling her face up to his. "In fact, I can show you just how much of a—"

Imogen ducked out from under his arms. At any other moment, her heart would be racing and she'd be breathless from his deliberate charm. Not now. Not in light of all he'd shared.

Alex released her so suddenly that she careened sideways then quickly righted herself. "You'll quote Shakespeare and dream the words of romantic poets." His gaze took her in from the top of her shamefully crimson head to the tips of her slippers, and then back up once more. "Yet you'd be better served if you stayed the hell away from me, Imogen. Have Primly for your husband."

Pain knifed through her. "You don't mean that."

"I do," he said, the merciless edge to his words sharper than any blade. "You've had your heart broken by Montrose. Any of this hero worship you'd heap upon me is not deserved. The only reason I came tonight was at the bequest of my sister."

Oh, God. She shook her head, incapable of getting words out past the emotion clogging her throat.

"Yes," he said with a bluntness that made her flinch. "The only reason I shared my . . . past . . ." he faltered over those words ". . . with you was so you might realize why I've become the man I am." Alex stalked over. "Do you know why I've been such a, how did you refer to it, doting brother?" He planted his hands on her shoulders, forcing her gaze up to his. "Because my brother, the revered marquess, has tired of my gaming, whoring, and drinking." She flinched. "He threatened to cut me off if I did not do my brotherly duty. I've only ever cared about myself." He released her so suddenly, she staggered back a step.

"I don't believe that," she said softly. Did she try to convince herself or him?

"Then you're a fool and it is no wonder you were too naïve to see Montrose's true character."

Imogen jerked back, his words more painful than had he struck her. She'd come to know him too much in this time to not recognize that this display was nothing more than a mechanism to push her away, a desperate bid to protect himself from further hurts. "Don't do this," she pleaded.

"I'm not doing anything but providing the truth." With a sharp, perfunctory bow, he spun on his heel and left.

A tear slid down her cheek, the silence of the room her only company. God help her. She'd gone and fallen in love with Lord Alex Edgerton, a man so determined to keep the walls up about his heart, he could never, *would* never, love her in return.

Chapter 13

*A*lex sat on the sofa in the library of his brother's townhouse, cloaked in the thick, dark silence of the early morning hours, head buried in his hands. Even with his abrupt departure from Imogen at Lady Ferguson's ball five hours past, a riot of emotions still churned through him.

He loved her. A hiss escaped his lungs, the slight exhalation of it as it burst from his lips the only sound in the dead of night.

Why are you doing this . . . ?

A lady once betrothed to a duke, now courted by an honorable earl, deserved far more than Lord Alex Edgerton, the broken and battered second son who'd been told with an enduring frequency of his unworthiness. First from the sire who'd given him life and then in all those countless women who took him to bed, wanting nothing more than the pleasure of his body. And those meaningless entanglements had been enough.

Until Imogen.

"May I come in?"

He snapped his head up. "I didn't hear you enter," he said, his voice gruff from the tumult of his emotions and the embarrassment of being caught unawares by his ever-perfect older brother.

Gabriel shoved the door closed behind him, then strode over. Then in a manner eerily reminiscent to an exchange that had taken place in this very room just recently, Gabriel paused at the foot of his seat. Alex reached for the full bottle of brandy and the empty glass alongside it. His brother covered his hand with his own, staying the movement. "You don't want that."

He did. Desperately. So he might find a liquid resolve. "What the hell do you know of it?" A wealth of questions buried within the one. At one time Gabriel had known. With the passage of time, he'd forgotten what they'd shared.

"If you truly wanted it, you'd have consumed nearly half the bottle. As it is, it's been untouched."

Alex tightened his fingers about the rim of his glass, hard enough to almost shatter the tumbler. He lightened his grip, damning his brother for being astute, seeing everything, and yet at the same time, seeing nothing. "What the hell do you want?"

"May I?" he motioned to the seat beside Alex.

"Surely the powerful marquess needn't ask permission to be seated in his own library." Did he imagine the spasm of pain to contort Gabriel's face? He scoffed. In spite of his protestations in their earlier conversation, Gabriel had ceased being human the moment the devil had taken him under his wing and provided tutelage to the revered heir.

Wordlessly, his elder brother flicked the tails of his jacket and claimed a seat. Gabriel swiped the bottle of brandy and made use of Alex's untouched glass to pour himself a drink. "You certainly left Society talking last evening with your showing at Forbidden Pleasures," he said without preamble.

Alex's public defense of Imogen would, of course, have been remarked upon and fast become fodder for the gossips. However, he'd not believed his exchange with Rutland would have circulated with such rapidity. Rather, he'd hoped it wouldn't. "The lady is a friend of our sister's," he said, in a bid to protect the truth of Imogen's hold upon him. "Then, I'd not expect you to understand matters of loyalty."

Gabriel winced and yet had proved far more resilient through the years. "I hardly expect it should matter to you what one such as Rutland says of the lady."

"It doesn't." The lie was automatic. He rolled his shoulders.

"Yet you defended her." His brother took a slow, deliberate sip. "Out of the lady's connection to Chloe?" Skepticism underscored the question.

A volatile force of emotion brought Alex to his feet. "Is there a question there?" His brother arched an eyebrow. "Rutland is a master manipulator," he said defensively. "He'd have the *ton* believe there is more there than actually is." *Liar.*

Ever imperial and unaffected, Gabriel leaned back in his seat. "Perhaps." He draped an arm along the back of the leather sofa. Of course, he'd not let the matter be. "I'm sure it was merely gossip and lies that claimed you'd defended the lady's beauty." A wry smile pulled at the other man's lips. "Though, the gentleman, doth protest too much, methinks."

He'd grown accustomed to a world in which Gabriel didn't know his interests or hopes or fears. Yet, for everything that had come to pass, he still remembered Alex's love of Shakespeare. A flush burned his neck. "You take the same twisted glee as our great sire in ferreting out one's weakness, but you're wrong on this score. I do not care for Imogen Moore." *I love her.* Two very, very different sentiments.

Gabriel went still, a flash of pain sparked in his eyes. "Is that truly how you see me? As an extension of our father?"

Bloody hell, he did not wish to have this discussion again with his brother. Dredging up their dark past was futile. No words could put to rights the rift between them. "We've already said everything there is to say about our . . ." His lip peeled back in a sneer. ". . . *father.*"

Gabriel surged to his feet. With a furious step, he stalked over and planted himself before Alex. Of like height, he stuck his face close. "Do you think you're the only one who suffered? Do you believe that when he took me under his tutelage I was somehow spared from his viciousness?" For the first time since he'd been a young, angry boy forgotten by his elder brother, hero, and protector, a niggling of doubt twisted about his brain. "I wasn't," he said with an almost gleeful delight in correcting Alex's erroneous supposition. "I was still a victim of his abuse. I still bore the blunt of his fist, his hand, or that damned birch rod whenever I faltered in the lessons he imparted."

If those words were truth, then it would mean everything he'd believed these nearly two decades had been wrong. He shook his head dumbly. No. The world would cease to make sense if his brother spoke the truth.

"Yes," Gabriel spoke in a deadened tone that could only come from another who'd shared in the hell of Alex's youth. He scoffed. "Come, you are smart, surely you noted the attention Father showed you after he'd separated us and began grooming me for the role of marquess?"

With a confounding sluggishness, he ran through the childhood years, rolled past the bitterness, resentment, and pain he carried at his brother's defection. As a small child, the beatings handed out had occurred with a shocking frequency. They'd never stopped.

"I couldn't stop him completely, Alex." Gabriel rubbed his chest as though in pain. "I was never that strong and in my inability to do so, I became the failure you've found me to be." He met his gaze square on. "But you were never the only one to know that pain. I don't want you to believe you were different or less worthy merely because of your position of birth. Chloe, Philippa." Gabriel sucked in a jagged breath and then his face tightened. He shook his head as though unable to revisit the horrors known by even the young Edgerton girls. "He'd have taken a piece of your flesh regardless, because that is what monsters do."

The world dipped and swayed and Alex found purchase on the edge of a winged back chair. "You protected me." He didn't recognize the hoarse declaration as his own.

Color filled his brother's face. "Don't have me be a hero. I'm not. If I was, I would have stopped him, maintained your friendship, cared for Chloe and Philippa, and . . ." His words trailed off and he dragged a palm over his face. "I've not come to again raise memories of our past. The day he died, I swore I'd never again mention his name." He cast a hungry look back at the bottle of brandy atop the table and it occurred to Alex just how great the demons Gabriel himself battled were.

Alex held his hand out, calling his brother's attention back away from those spirits that would not truly provide any escape from the past. He knew as one who'd tried. "I . . ." He cleared his throat, which was tight with emotions too long buried.

Gabriel placed his hand in Alex's and held tight. "I know, Alex. I love you, too." His brother stared at their clasped hands and then, with the alacrity of one who'd been schooled in concealing any and all emotion, released Alex's fingers. "Your Lady Imogen," he began.

A grin pulled at the right corner of Alex's lips. "You're unrelenting."

"You may believe she'd be better with a titled gentleman, but she nearly had the Duke of Montrose. And what has that brought her?" The words were eerily reminiscent to those spoken by the lady herself in Ferguson's office. His brother coughed into his hand. "I'll leave you to your thoughts."

He nodded. "Gabriel, I'm—"

"Don't," he commanded, cutting into a futile apology that could never right the wrongs done by Alex, the lies he'd allowed himself to believe, and worse, for consigning his brother to the same loathed column as their father. Gabriel patted him awkwardly on the shoulder and then with stiff, jerky movements started for the door. At the entrance, he froze and turned back around. "There could be far worse things than giving your heart to a respectable lady who'd take care of that love."

And with that, he left.

Alex's shoulders sagged. He'd spent years hating his brother for having abandoned him, when in truth Gabriel had sought to shelter him, to hold the marquess's attention for his own and, through that redirect, the madman's ire away from his younger siblings. He was humbled by the shame of his own self-absorption, for failing to see the truth that had always been there, if he'd only glimpsed past his own self-centeredness to see the truths painted before him.

Another knock sounded at the door. Woodenly, he picked up his head.

"May I come in?" Without waiting for permission, Chloe slipped inside the library.

He mustered a grin for his youngest sister. "Of course you intended to do so regardless."

She smiled. "Indeed." Then she winced, touching her fingers to her temple. Alarmed, he hurried over but she merely waved him off. "It will take more than a megrim to weaken me." He believed that. In all she'd endured and triumphed through, she was stronger than any gentleman he knew.

He motioned her over. "Sit."

With a sigh, she walked slowly over and then sank into the wide leather sofa he'd occupied earlier. The old folds of the seat swallowed her diminutive form. In this moment, she may as well have been the same girl who'd dogged his footsteps and made a disastrous habit of imitating her older, incorrigible brother's poor behaviors. Chloe drew her knees up and dropped her chin atop the top of her thick, modest cotton wrapper. "I overheard your discussion with Gabriel."

She still possessed that bothersome habit of listening at keyholes. "Did you?" he asked dryly, which of course indicated she'd heard mention of a certain fiery beauty who'd slipped into his deadened heart and breathed life back into the once useless organ.

She nodded. "About, Imogen." Chloe chewed her lower lip. "Well, all of it really. But particularly the part about Imogen." Unrest stirred in her blue eyes, trained upon her knees. "I don't care to speak of him."

He fastened his gaze at her arms looped about her knees. "I know."

With a flounce of her curls, she dispelled dark mentions of their evil sire. "Imogen."

Unbidden, another grin turned his lips, her name alone filling him with a lightness he'd not believed himself capable of.

"Oh, dear you are quite in love." Chloe lowered her legs in a flurry of white skirts. "I daresay you've not told her."

"No, I've not told her," he murmured. In fact, he'd done just the opposite, really. A pressure squeezed like a vise about his lungs. When she'd come to him with words about the man she believed him to be, he'd pushed her away, all but inviting her to accept Primly's suit.

"Humph."

Alex was desperate enough that he'd talk to his minx of a sister about romance. "'Humph' what?"

With a wispy wave of her hand, she said, "I'd expect a legendary rogue such as the notorious Lord Alex would have a good deal more finesse on matters of the heart."

He frowned. If she believed the terms *rogue* and *matters of the heart* could be paired, then he and Gabriel had a good deal more to worry about in terms of their young, romantic sister.

Chloe rested her fingers on his knee. "You need to tell her, Alex. You need to tell her, or you'll always regret that you did not."

He clenched and unclenched his jaw. "She'd be better off with Primly."

An inelegant snort spilled past her lips. "Poor, hopelessly shy Primly?" She gave a shake of her blonde curls. "Why, because he's an earl?"

Because he was honorable and moral when Alex was not, and yet . . .

"It doesn't matter," she spoke in quiet tones, echoing the thoughts filtering through his mind. "It matters not that you're a second born son and he's an earl or a duke, or Prinny himself. She wants to be loved. As we all do," she murmured that last part more to herself. Then she gave her head a firm shake, as though dispelling any thoughts of love as it pertained to her own happiness. "You love her," she repeated.

The viselike pressure about his lungs lessened and he could at last breathe again. For the first time. He loved Imogen, and in a short time she'd opened his eyes to the man he truly was and, more important to the man he wished to be, a man worthy of her love.

Chloe hopped to her feet and then touched a finger to her temple at the suddenness of the movement. "Splendid." She patted him on the head as though he were a well-behaved spaniel. "I'd suspected all you two needed was a bit of a push." With an uncharacteristic slowness to her step, she walked over to the door.

Then her words registered. "What?"

She froze in the threshold. "Surely you didn't believe your being thrown together was a mere coincidence." With a saucy wink, she slipped from the room. "Not much of a rogue . . ." The remainder of her words were lost to the corridor.

By God, his sister had played matchmaker for him? A real chuckle, not the practiced cynical one he'd employed through the years, rumbled in his chest. "Not much of a rogue, indeed," he said into the quiet of the room.

"Oh, and Alex."

"Bloody hell," he groused. His heart thudded at the unexpected appearance of his sister once more. "Shouldn't you be abed? Your head—"

"Is vastly improved." She grinned. "I just thought I should mention I've read a number of scandal sheets and heard from the maid, Lucy, who is dating the footman, Terrance, whose sister is employed by the Earl of—"

"Chloe," he said, unable to quell the edge of impatience.

"Er, right, yes. Well, servants do talk, and the Earl of Primly's servants have whispered that the gentleman intends to offer for Imogen." With a slight, mocking curtsy she turned on her heel and took her leave.

His heart thumped a panicked rhythm inside his chest. Primly intended to offer for her. And why wouldn't he? But the other man would not simply make his offer, not until Alex first spoke to her. His gaze found the ormolu clock atop the fireplace mantel. He struggled to bring the numbers into focus in the dimly lit room. As long as he'd known Primly, the man had been a respectable figure who adhered to propriety and conventions and at this fashionable hour, was likely there even now with Imogen.

Squaring his jaw, Alex started for the door. She could not accept Primly. Not until Alex himself told her the words in his heart.

He loved her.

Chapter 14

*I*mogen trailed her fingertips over the green leather volume of Shakespeare's *Romeo and Juliet*, recalling her trip to the theater, Alex at her side, whispering words of the Bard into her ear while caressing her palm. The actions of a rogue, and yet not.

Her eyes snagged upon a verse and she fixed on those apropos words.

Is love a tender thing? It is too rough,
Too rude, too boist'rous; and it pricks like thorn.

Last evening, he'd positioned himself at her side, weathering the gossip as she and her sister and her former betrothed were placed on display like an exhibit at the Royal Museum. Those actions were not those of a gentleman who did not care. Nor did his insistence that he'd merely come at Chloe's urging bear any credence. Perhaps in the immediacy of his departure but not now. Imogen set aside her book and reached for literature she abhorred before all others. She perused the scandal sheets that had cast aspersions on the heartless words Alex had flung at her last evening.

A certain Lord AE publicly declared his regard for a certain Lady IM before a collection of guests gathered at a notorious club. In addition to mentioning the lady's beauty and intelligence, the gentleman quite honorably defended . . .

Etc., etc., etc. . . .

A wistful smile played about her lips. Surely those were not the words or actions of a disinterested gentleman who'd danced attendance upon her solely for his sister's benefit?

"The audacity of the man," her mother cried from the doorway, bringing Imogen's attention up. She sighed at the unexpected and undesired appearance of her overdramatic mama. "Mother," she began, knowing very well the lady who loved the scandal sheets, mayhap more than her own children, had certainly seen mention of Alex and her name.

The countess brandished a copy of one scandal sheet or another and waved it about. "Lord Alex Edgerton!"

"What of Lord Alex Edgerton?" she asked patiently.

In a wholly un-countess-like move, her mother all but sprinted over and waved the page before Imogen's face. "He . . . he . . . fought about you. Over you, my dear."

"He?" She arched an eyebrow.

Mother's eyebrows shot to her hairline. "Surely you've read the scandal pages." Then, with a pained groan, she took in Imogen's reading material. "Shakespeare? My dear, I do not know how I so failed you that you'd be devoted to that, that drivel when there is far more important business to attend to."

"And by business, do you mean gossip?"

"Precisely." Mother slapped the page against her other palm. Her frown deepened as she realized her response. She gave a frantic little shake of her head. "Matters of the *ton* are not gossip. They are the matters that rule our world."

"Gossip," she felt inclined to point out. Having been victim to too many gossip columns, she'd be content to send every last writer of the pieces revered by the peers off to the devil to burn in a fiery inferno.

"I shan't debate the explanation of it with you, Imogen."

"Denotation," she amended under her breath.

Mother tossed the scandal sheet atop Imogen's copy of *Romeo and Juliet*. Poor Mr. Shakespeare, he'd likely be crafting a villainous character in the woman's honor for such a slight. "Lord. Alex. Edgerton."

Oh, dear, when she punctuated her words in that manner, it spoke volumes of her upset. Imogen plucked at the fabric of her skirts. "Is that a question?" A statement?

"He has declared his interest in you."

Her heart sped up. "He's done no such thing." Only if the scandal pages were to be believed, and surely some of them bore the hint of truth, then he had, in fact, done so, in a very public manner.

"What of Lord Primly?"

She angled her head.

An aggravated sigh escaped the countess. "Lord Primly. The earl. The gentleman who would—"

A knock sounded at the door. Their gazes swung as one to the flushed face of Lord Primly and the impressively composed butler. "The Earl of Primly," he announced, a sheepish glance spared for Imogen.

The earl's pale cheeks turned red at their silent scrutiny and then Mother flew across the room. "My lord, what an honor to see you." His color heightened under the woman's gushing tone.

He caught Imogen's gaze and, if possible, his color flared once more. "It is an honor to be here," he murmured. Not a hint of a stammer.

Her heart dipped somewhere into the vicinity of her stomach. Oh, goodness, he'd asked her to consider his suit, spoken very plainly about the possibility of more between them, and yet she'd only been able to think of Alex and their meeting in Lord Ferguson's office.

"I shall leave you to your visit," Mother said with a giddy smile. She cast a glance back at Imogen and then slipped from the room, leaving her and Lord Primly—alone.

Very alone.

Imogen looked to her maid quietly embroidering in the corner. But for her maid. Thank God for Lucy. Her feet twitched with the desire to take flight. Lord Primly hung back by the doorway, hesitantly shifting back and forth on his feet. Belatedly, she remembered her manners. "Won't you come in, my lord?"

He lurched forward in long, loping strides and she could not help but compare him to the man her heart wanted, a man whose demons would surely never allow him to open his heart. Yet, there was the exchange between him and Rutland . . .

"Would you care for refreshments?" she asked when they'd taken places across from each other.

"No refreshments." He spoke as though he'd wadded a kerchief in his mouth.

She eyed him askance. "My lord, are you all—?"

"I'd asked you to think on a match between us."

That not-so-veiled suggestion he'd made at Lady Ferguson's last evening now became a formal offer. Imogen's mouth went dry.

A bead of moisture dotted the man's high brow. "I am here to offer you marriage."

Her heart already somewhere in her stomach, sank all the way to the bottom, landing at her toes. *Need you be surprised, silly?* But for dropping to a knee in the midst of Lady Ferguson's ballroom and putting to her an offer of marriage,

Lord Primly had been abundantly clear in his intentions. In him, she would likely have a quiet, companionable union, however devoid of passion and love it might happen to be. Unwittingly, her gaze fell to the scandal sheet.

"I read about Lord Alexander."

That brought her head up. "Oh." Surely there was no suitable response to such an admission.

The morning's rays now glinted off the earl's perspiring brow. He yanked out a handkerchief and dabbed at his forehead. "I-I'll not disparage Edgerton in my bid to make you my countess." With those words, the gentleman rose mightily in her estimation, as she saw in him one of the rare good souls amidst their jaded and soulless world. "But I will promise to c-care for you and you'll want for nothing and . . ."

Imogen placed a hand upon his, staying his words.

Those bug-like blue eyes went enormous in his face, as though scandalized at the touch of a lady, even if the lady was one he'd just put a formal offer of marriage to. "My lady?" he squeaked, yanking his hand back as though scorched.

Alexander would never be so scandalized by a gentle caress. Instead, he'd likely have ordered Lucy from the room and then taken her lips under his. Regret squeezed at her heart. Why wouldn't he accept the gift of her love? "I wanted to thank you for the honor, my lord." Hope flared in his eyes. "But it would not be right for me to wed you."

His shoulders sagged. "Because you love Edgerton?" He directed his question to the floor.

A pang of remorse pulled at her heart. "Because you are a good, kind, and honorable man who deserves a woman who will love you." And she could not be that woman, not when her heart and whole soul belonged to another. "I would make you a deplorable hostess."

At those decisive words, a sad smile turned his lips up at the corners. "I barely stammer when you're near. You'd make me a better host."

For Society's ill opinion of Lord Primly, she came to appreciate the tenacity of the gentleman. She opened her mouth, but he cut into any further protestations on her part. "What if he will not wed you? Would you then consider—?"

"No," she said with a gentle firmness. "You deserve more than that, my lord." At one time, immediately after Montrose's betrayal, she'd have likely accepted a passionless union based on comfort. Not anymore. She deserved more. Just as the earl did. "You'll find love. I am sure of it."

"I'd settle for a wife who I didn't stammer before," he mumbled.

She suspected as much, which was one of the reasons she'd not wed him.

Lord Primly beat his hand against his thigh and eyed the scandal sheet open upon the table before them. "I know what they say of Edgerton." She straightened her spine. "But I have always liked the gentleman." He picked his head up and gave her a sheepish smile. "One of the only men at university who didn't have fun at my expense."

Another pang pulled at her heart and she detested all those who'd made the kindly man's life a misery, loving Alex all the more for having once been a friend to him.

He rocked back and forth on the balls of his feet. She must be madder than a madman running the halls of Bedlam to turn down such a safe, practical offer. "Thank you, my lord," she said softly.

He bowed. "My lady." With that, he took his leave.

Seated on the squabs of his carriage, Alex withdrew his watch fob for surely the hundredth time and consulted the time on his pocket watch. With a curse, he stuffed it back into his pocket, then tugged the red velvet curtain aside. He peered at the clogged roadways. The cheerful hothouse blooms on the opposite seat stared mockingly at him.

At this rate, Primly would have put his offer to Imogen, married her, and spirited her off to the country. He growled and banged on the roof of the carriage and his driver pulled hard on the reins of the team. "Bloody hell," he muttered as the jerky stop tossed him against the side of the carriage. The flowers tumbled to the floor.

"Lord Alexander?" the driver, James, called.

Alex shoved the door open and leaped out of the conveyance. "I'll walk the remainder of the way." He grunted as the jarring movement coursed up his leg.

The liveried servant adjusted his cap and eyed the busy streets skeptically. "You're certain, Lord Alexander?" He glanced about the crowded streets and then to Alex.

"I am." With that, he started along the fashionable streets of Mayfair, onward toward . . . He cursed and spun around and nearly collided with James. The man gave a lopsided grin and held up the forgotten bouquet of white roses.

"You forgot your flowers, my lord."

Dismissing, the curious stares from passersby trained on him, he accepted the flowers with a murmured thanks and strode down the street once more. Dread stirred in his chest and built slowly as he imagined Primly, even now, dropping to a chivalrous knee and offering Imogen his name, and worse, his heart. Alex picked up his pace, weaving between the throngs of lords and ladies out at the fashionable hour. He should have arrived earlier. He'd not required the flowers. Only he'd wanted the flowers. After what the Duke of Montrose had stolen from her, Imogen deserved sonnets and flowers and love and more. He gritted his teeth so hard pain radiated up his jawline. What good would his meager offerings be if she'd already accepted Primly's damned suit? She could not have. And God help Alex for being the bastard he was, for if she did, he wanted her to break it off with the other man, throw him over, and have Alex . . .

Panic built in time to the frantic beat of his steps and he lengthened his stride as the white stucco finish of her family's townhouse came into focus. Alex sprinted the remaining distance. He bounded up the handful of steps just as the front door opened.

Lord Primly stepped out.

The flowers slipped from Alex's fingers and fell in a thump on the stone stoop. *Ah God.*

An always entirely too cheerful Primly grinned. "Hullo, Edgerton. So good to see you." No, it wasn't. It was bloody torture seeing the other man here, knowing what, rather *who*, had brought him here.

"Primly," he squeezed out past a tight throat. "A pleasure," he lied. He wanted to hate the man. He truly did.

The man, who'd have Imogen for himself, dropped his gaze. "Oh, y-you've dropped your f-flowers," he said, a smile in his voice. He picked them up and held them out.

Alex accepted the wilted bouquet in a confounded quiet. Did the gentleman *truly* realize what brought Alex here?

Surely he did not. For Primly's smile widened as he tipped the brim of his hat. "Good day, Edgerton."

Struggling for breath, Alex spun to the still open door and entered behind the graying butler. He shifted the rapidly wilting, crushed blooms in his hands and fished around the front of his jacket for his card. "Lord Alex Edgerton to see Lady I-Imogen," he said with a newfound appreciation for how difficult it was for Primly to go through life in a constant state of anxiety. He shrugged out of his cloak and a servant rushed forward to relieve him of his burden.

The butler studied the card a moment and then motioned him forward. "Lady Imogen is receiving visitors in the drawing room."

His mouth dry, Alex fell into step behind the old servant, his mind curiously blank. What if she'd accepted Primly's offer? Agony gripped his chest. What if she saw the truth, that Alex was, in fact, the worthless bounder his father had always accused him of being? What if Gabriel and even Imogen herself had been wrong and she'd at last realized that he was unworthy . . . ?

The butler stopped before an opened door. "The Lord Alexander Edgerton," he announced.

Perched on the edge of her chair, with a book atop her lap, Imogen's mouth fell open in surprise. "Alex," she blurted. She hopped to her feet, her emerald-green skirts rustling noisily. The leather volume tumbled from her lap, falling noisily to the floor.

He stuck his rumpled offering out. "I've brought you these." Did that harsh, guttural tone belong to him?

She tipped her head at an endearing angle. "You—?"

Alex stalked over and spoke, cutting into her words. "I lied to you."

Imogen opened and closed her mouth several times and then called out to the maid in the corner. "Lucy, will you see to refreshments?" She gave the servant a pointed look. The young maid hopped to her feet and hurried from the room, closing the door partially behind her. "Alex, I—"

"I lied to you," he repeated. He dragged a hand through his hair. "I told you to accept Primly. I told you that I'd only attended Ferguson's ball at my sister's bequest. Both lies." He tossed the bouquet of flowers onto the rose inlay table and claimed her hands, raising them to his lips one at a time. "I was there because of you."

"I know that," she said softly. Did she? Could she truly know that as he'd sat at his clubs, he'd been ravaged inside at the idea of her facing down the cruel *ton* with no one but her empty-headed mother at her side?

"I'd intended to write you a sonnet." Her eyes lit with such pleased surprise, regret twisted in his belly. "But I'm rubbish at composing sonnets."

Imogen's lips twitched with a smile.

Alex picked the bouquet up and held it out to her.

"Doubt thou the stars are fire;
Doubt that the sun doth move;
Doubt truth to be a liar;
But never doubt I love."

Her lips parted on a small moue of surprise at the familiar lines of Shakespeare's verses.

Alex held her gaze, the brilliant blue of her eyes piercing him. "If you wed Primly, it will destroy me." Destroy him in ways his father never had managed. "He offered for you, didn't he?"

"He did."

Alex stared blankly down at the white roses. He'd lost her. "I see." Emotion climbed into his throat and threatened to choke him. He pressed his eyes closed, aware now more than ever how woefully inadequate he was—how undeserving.

"I don't believe you do." A soft caress upon his cheek brought his eyes open. "Not if you insist on keeping your eyes closed as you do."

"Did you accept his offer?" The moments since he'd asked that question passed with an agonizing slowness.

"I did not," she said at last. With an exaggerated sigh she claimed his face between her hands. "How could I ever accept his offer when I love you as I do?"

His throat worked spasmodically. "I believed he would be better for you. He could offer you the title of countess."

"Which I do not want."

"And a routine, staid life."

"Perfectly dull and boring."

Alex looped his arm about her waist and drew her close. "You crave passion and excitement, do you, Imogen?" he asked, lowering his mouth close to hers.

"No, Alex," her whispered reply froze him, their lips a hairsbreadth apart. "I crave only you."

He'd spent his entire life proving himself to be a shiftless bounder, an indolent rogue who cared about no one's pleasures but his own. Until this slender slip of a lady had shown him that he wanted more. "Then if you'll have me, I'd make you my wife." He wanted *her*.

Imogen leaned up on tiptoe and claimed his lips. He slanted his lips over hers, reacquainting himself with the soft, supple contours of her bow-shaped mouth. Alex drew back and she moaned in protest. "Is that a yes, love?"

A slow, saucy smile tipped her lips up in the corners. "That is a yes."

Epilogue

"*I*t seems dreadful giving it up," Lady Anne, the Countess of Stanhope, said on a beleaguered sigh to the group of ladies accompanying her down the crowded, cobbled London roads. "It has been such a part of our lives—"

The lady's sisters, Lady Katherine and Lady Aldora, paused to shoot her a dark look, quelling the remainder of those words. "Do hush, it is hardly fair to keep the item," Aldora scolded.

Walking beside the ladies, Imogen listened as the sisters debated the fate of a certain bauble. The item in question being the fabled heart of a duke pendant.

Anne bristled defensively. "I'm not saying we should keep it. Of course the pendant must find its way to some other young lady who might win the heart of her duke."

"Or the heart of her love," her twin sister, Katherine, murmured at her side.

Yes, the ladies, now joined together by bonds that moved beyond friendship, bonds of knowing true love, could all attest to the power of that heart pendant now carried in Aldora's reticule.

"She is here." Lady Aldora drew to a stop at the end of the pavement, eyeing the cluster of colorful tents at the end of Gypsy Hill.

"How do you know?" Lady Katherine asked, furrowing her brow as she took in the crowds littering the streets. The air rang with the peals of gypsy vendors hawking their wares.

"She knows because she has been here." The lovely blonde Countess of Stanhope clasped her hands to her chest. "She has met Bunică not once but twice, and we shall now meet her . . ."

As the excited young lady prattled on and on, Imogen stole a glance over her shoulder at the gentlemen trailing close after them. Her husband walked beside his friend, the Earl of Stanhope. Alex paused midsentence and looked questioningly at her. Imogen gave him a smile and he grinned in return. A contented sigh escaped her lips.

"Come along," Lady Aldora said and then set off through the crowds, picking her way down the street. The lady's sisters and their husbands followed along.

Imogen fell back. The lone unwed woman at her side eagerly eyed the street excitement with little interest or regard for the legendary pendant. She touched a hand to Chloe's.

The young lady startled and returned her attention to Imogen. She looked at her askance. "What—?"

"Surely you wish to wear the pendant, Chloe." Imogen looked over at Alex who stood back, allowing the young ladies their privacy.

Chloe snorted. "Surely I do not."

Imogen captured her other hand and gave them both a squeeze. "But you must want love for yourself."

Chloe ran her gaze over Imogen's face and then applied gentle pressure to her fingers. "Oh, Imogen. I knew you and Alex would be perfect together." Her lips twisted up in a wry smile. "I also knew you were both too bloody obstinate to ever see the truth before you." A mischievous twinkle lit the other woman's eyes. "You merely required a little help."

Imogen's mouth fell agape. "Why . . . why . . . ?" Why, her friend had played matchmaker with an ease most society matrons would have admired. Imogen widened her eyes. "Alex did not tell me."

Chloe squeezed her hands once more. "It is enough that you two found love." She looked over at Alex, now consulting his timepiece, and then she returned her attention to Imogen, the earlier light gone from her eyes. "My brother is a good man. I know that. And that is how I knew he'd make you an ideal match. But there are no others. No others I'd trust beyond my brothers . . ." Her words trailed off.

Regret pulled at Imogen. When her own heart had been shattered by her sister's betrayal, Chloe had forced her to hold onto the dream of love and magic and romance, and yet . . . She should not hold even a dash of any of those sentiments for herself.

Then, as though she'd merely imagined the other woman's grim solemnity, Chloe's face lit with a smile. "Enough of this seriousness. With Alex wedded and my mother returned, she'll be scheming to marry her remaining children off." She wrinkled her nose. "And therefore I intend to enjoy my time with the gypsies. Mayhap they have some other manner of magic for one such as me." With a wink, she hurried ahead after the twin sisters who lingered beside a red tent, where a coarse vendor peddled his wares, a monkey atop his shoulder.

A pair of firm, reassuring, and now familiar hands settled about her shoulders. "What is it, love?" Alex whispered against her ear.

She accepted the comfort of his touch, all the while staring after Chloe. "I am worried about her." Even being thrown over and betrayed by her former love who'd gone and wed her sister, Imogen had still clung to a sliver of hope of happiness for herself. Chloe's abject hopelessness regarding her own happiness chilled her.

Alex's firm lips tipped down at the corners as he followed her gaze to his sister, laughing at something Lady Anne had just said to her. The clear, tinkling sound carried over to them and yet . . . "She will be all right." He spoke as if more to himself.

How could he be so certain? Imogen chewed her lower lip, worrying. How could he know . . . ?

"I know because I believe in love," he murmured. His breath fanned her cheek. "You taught me that love is indeed very real and, more importantly, to trust in giving myself over to the power of those sentiments. You saved me, Imogen," he said simply. "And believing that now as I do, how can I ever truly believe a woman such as Chloe will not know love?" Alex raised her gloved hands to his mouth one at a time, pressing his lips against her knuckles.

"But—"

"Do you believe in love?" he charged.

"How can I not?" How, when her every day was brighter, her joy greater, her heart fuller because of him?

"Then trust, Imogen." Taking her by the hand, he tucked it into the crook of his elbow. "Now come along. I daresay a lady who quotes Shakespeare and dreams of romance would relish being here at Gypsy Hill."

Imogen leaned close to her husband. *Trust*. He'd have her trust that Chloe would be well. He spoke with the same bold assurance of a man who'd found love and believed. He credited her with having opened his eyes. And yet, as they set after Chloe, she acknowledged the truth—they'd saved each other.

The End

Heart of a Duke series

continues with

Loved by a Duke
To Love a Lord
The Heart of a Scoundrel
To Wed His Christmas Lady
To Trust a Rogue
The Lure of a Rake
To Woo a Widow
To Redeem a Rake
One Winter With a Baron
To Enchant a Wicked Duke
Beguiled by a Baron
To Tempt a Scoundrel

Turn the page for an excerpt of *Loved by a Duke*!

Chapter 1

London, England
21 April 1816

 ady Daisy Meadows was invisible.

Oh, she hadn't always been a shiftless, shapeless figure overlooked by all. In fact, she'd been quite the bane of her poor mother and father's existence, and prone to all manner of mischief, since a young girl had about as little hope of being made Queen of England as accomplishing the whole invisibility feat. And yet, she'd managed it with a remarkable finesse, through no help of her own. She could point to the precise moment in time when she ceased to be.

She plucked the copy of *The Times* from the rose-inlaid, mahogany table and scanned the words on the front page; so familiar she'd already committed them to memory.

Duke of C in the market for his duchess, thrown over by the Lady AA, etc., etc.,

Offended by the blasted page, Daisy stuck her tongue out at the mocking words and threw the paper onto the table. *Thwack!* "Market for a duchess," she muttered under her breath. "As though he's hunting for a prime piece of horseflesh."

The Duke of C. None other than the illustrious, sought after, Duke of Crawford. Sought after by all . . . She glanced down at the page once more. Well, not all. After all, the then Lady Anne Adamson had rejected his suit in favor of the roguish Earl of Stanhope. The fool.

A fool Daisy was indebted to. But a fool nonetheless.

With a growl of annoyance she grabbed for the embroidery frame. She picked up the needle and jammed it through the screen with such zeal she jabbed the sharp tip into the soft flesh of her index finger. "Blast." She popped the wounded digit into her mouth and sucked the drop of blood. When she'd become invisible, she'd also taken to embroidering. She had been doing so for nearly seven years. She was as rubbish at it as she was at winning the heart of a certain duke.

With needle in hand, and greater care on her part, she pulled it through the outline of the heart . . . she wrinkled her brow . . . or, it was intended to be a heart. Now it bore the hint of a sad circle with a slight dip in the middle. She tugged the needle through once more with entirely too much zeal and stuck her finger again. "Double blast."

Giving up on the hope of distraction, she tossed the frame aside where it landed upon the damning page with a quiet *thwack*. She hopped to her feet then made her way over to the hearth. A small fire cast soothing warmth into the chilled room. She rubbed her palms together and contemplated the flickering flames.

It shouldn't matter what the scandal sheets reported about a certain duke in the market for a wife. She'd known it was an inevitability he would wed and had long ago accustomed herself to that sad, sorry truth that it would not be her but instead a flawless English beauty such as the Lady Anne. There had been whispers of a fabled heart pendant given by a gypsy and worn by the lady to win the heart of a duke. Nothing more than whispers from romantic ladies who believed in such silly talismans. It wouldn't have mattered if Lady Anne had been in possession of an armoire full of magic pendants. With her golden blonde curls and a remarkably curved figure, she could have had any duke, marquess, or in the lady's case—earl, she wanted. Unlike plump, unfortunately curved Daisy. To Auric, the 8th Duke of Crawford she was just as invisible to him as she was to everyone.

She picked her gaze up and stared at her reflection in the enormous, gold mirror. A wry grin formed on her too large lips. Odd, how a lady cursed with dark brown hair and a shocking amount of freckles, and of such a *plump* form should ever achieve the whole invisibility feat, and yet she had. "Now, I," she said to the creature with enormous, brown eyes. "I require some enchanted object." Nothing short of a gypsy's charm would help her win Auric's stubborn, blind heart.

Shuffling footsteps sounded in the hall, calling her attention. Her mother stood framed in the doorway gazing with an empty stare at the parlor, as though she'd entered a foreign world and didn't know how to escape it. It was the same blank look and wan expression she'd worn since they'd learned of Lionel.

Her brother. Her protector. Defender. And champion. Smiling and tweaking her nose one day. The next, lost in the most brutal manner imaginable. With his senseless death, he'd taken her parents' only happiness with them, and with his aching absence, left her invisible.

"Mother." There was a pain that would never go away in knowing, as the living child, Daisy could never restore happiness to her mother's world.

The marchioness blinked several times. "Daisy?"

"Yes." As in the woman's daughter and only surviving child.

"I . . ." Mother touched her fingertips to her temple as though she had a vicious megrim. "I have a bit of a headache." She glanced about the room. "Is Aur—?"

"He is not here," Daisy interrupted. Following her husband's death two years earlier, the Duke of Crawford had become the only person her mother left the privacy of her darkened chambers for. In his presence, she somehow found traces of the mother, hostess, and person she'd been before her, nay *their*, world had been torn asunder.

"He is not," her mother repeated, furrowing her brow. With his visits, it was as though the cloak of misery she'd donned these years would lift, and the woman would show traces of the proper hostess she'd been once upon a lifetime ago. But with his departure, she'd settle into the fog of despair once again.

"No, Mama," she said gentling her tone as though speaking to a fractious mare. Auric hadn't been 'round in nearly a month. Three weeks and six days to be precise. But who was counting? "Surely you do not expect he'll visit forever?" There was no reason for him to do so. "He'll take a duchess soon." She hated the way her heart tugged painfully at that truth.

A flash of lucidity lit the marchioness' gray-blue eyes. "Do not be rude, Daisy."

"I'm not being rude." She was being truthful. Even as she longed to be the reason for his coming 'round, she'd long ago accepted that his visits were out of a ducal obligation to the dear friends of his late parents. And through it all, Daisy remained invisible. "His visits are merely an obligatory social call, Mother."

"I can't think when you speak like that." Her mother clenched her eyes tight and rubbed her temples, pressing her fingers into the skin. "I . . ."

Remorse flooded her and she swept across the room. "Shh." She took her mother by the shoulders and gave her a gentle squeeze. "You should rest."

The older woman nodded. "Yes. Yes. That is a very good idea. I should rest." She turned away woodenly and left in a sea of black, bombazine skirts. The only time she replaced her mourning attire was when she was forced out into Society with her still unwed daughter.

With a sigh, Daisy wandered back to the hearth and stared down into the orange-red flames. The fire snapped and hissed noisily in the quiet of the room. When she'd been a small girl, she'd loved to hop. She would jump on two feet, until she'd discovered the thrill of that unsteady one-footed hop. Then her mother had discovered her hopping and put a subsequent end to any such behavior.

At least when there was a hint of a possibility of Mother being near. Now, with her father gone, dead in his sleep not even two years ago, and a mother who'd ceased to note her existence, Daisy would quite gladly trade her current state for that overbearing, oft-scolding mother.

She gently tugged up the hem of her gown and jumped on her two slippered feet. A smile pulled at her lips as the familiar thrill of the forbidden filled her. Even if it was only the forbidden that existed in her mind, from a time long ago. Did she even remember how to hop? She'd not done so in . . . she searched her mind. Seven years? Surely not. Entirely too long for any person to not do something as enjoyable as jump or hop.

Daisy held her arms out at her side and experimented with a tentative hop. She chewed her lips. Boots had been ever so much more conducive to this manner of enjoyable business. "How utterly silly," she mumbled to herself. It was silly. Quite juvenile, really. And yet, despite knowing that and all the lessons of propriety ingrained into her, giddiness filled her chest. With a widening smile she hopped higher, catching her reflection in the mirror, a kind of testament to the fact that she was, in truth, visible. Still real. Still alive when the loved, cherished brother no longer was. "I am here," she said softly into the quiet of the ivory parlor. Daisy lifted her skirts higher and hopped up and down on one foot. Her loose chignon released several brown curls. They tumbled over her eye and she blew them back.

Ladies did not hop. Invisible ones, however, were permitted certain freedoms.

Her smile widened at the triviality of her actions. For many years, she'd been besieged with guilt for daring to smile or laugh when Lionel should never again do either. Eventually, she had. And along with guilt there was also some joy for the reminder that she was in fact—

"Ahem, the Duke of Crawford."

Daisy came down hard on her ankle and, with a curse, crumpled before the hearth. Her heartbeat sped up as she caught a glimpse of Auric's towering form, over the ivory satin sofa, at the entranceway. He wore his familiar ducal frown. However, the usually stoic, unflappable peer hovered blinking at her in her pile of sea foam green skirts.

She mustered a smile. "Hullo." She made to shove herself to her feet.

He was across the room in three long strides. "What are you doing?" Not: *How are you?* Not: *Are you all right?* And certainly not: *My love, please don't be injured.*

She winged an eyebrow upward. "Oh, you know, I'm merely sitting here admiring the lovely fire." His frown deepened.

Then in one effortless movement, he scooped her up and set her on her feet. A thrill of warmth charged through her at his strong hands upon her person. "Are you hurt?"

Well, there, a bit belated, but she supposed, better late than never. "I'm fine," she assured him. Her maid appeared in the doorway. "Agnes, will you see to refreshments?"

The young woman, who'd been with her for almost six years, turned on her heel and hurried to see to her mistress' bidding. Agnes had come to know, just like every other servant, peer, and person, that there was no danger to Daisy's reputation where the Duke of Crawford was concerned.

She took a tentative step, testing for injury.

"You'd indicated you were unhurt," he spoke in a disapproving tone, as though perturbed at the idea of her being hurt.

Goodness, she'd not want to go and bother him by being injured. "I am all right," she replied automatically. Then, "What are you doing here?" Mortified heat burned her cheeks at the boldness of her own question.

He gave her an indecipherable look.

"Not that you're not welcome to visit." *Shut up this instant, Daisy Laurel.* "You are of course, welcome." He continued to study her in that inscrutable way of his. Sometime between charming young boy of sixteen and now, he'd perfected ducal haughtiness. Annoyed by his complete mastery of his emotions, she slipped by him and claimed a seat on the ivory sofa. "What I intended to say is," *I*, "my mother missed your visits."

There was a slight tightening at the corners of his lips. Beyond that, however, he gave no indication that he either cared, remembered, or worried about the Marchioness of Roxbury.

She sat back in her seat. "Would you care to sit?" *Or would you rather stand there glowering in that menacing manner of yours?*

He sat. And still glowered in that menacing manner of his. "What were you doing?"

Daisy blinked at this crack in his previously cool mask. "What was I doing?"

"Prior to your fall." Auric jerked his chin toward the hearth. "It appeared as though you were," he peered down the length of his aquiline nose. "Hopping." The grinning Auric of his youth would have challenged her to a jumping competition. This hard person he'd become spoke to the man who found inane amusements, well . . . *inane.*

She trilled a forced laugh. "Oh, hopping." Daisy gave a wave of her hand that she hoped conveyed "what-a-silly -idea-whyever-would-I-do-anything-as-childlike-as-hop?" To give her fingers something to do, she grabbed for her embroidery frame and cautiously eyed the offending needle.

Auric shifted in the King Louis XIV chair taking in the frame in her hands. "You don't embroider."

No, by the weak rendering upon the frame, he'd be correct in that regard. For as deplorable as she was, she really quite enjoyed it. Her stitchery was some-thing she did for herself. It was a secret enjoyment that belonged to her and no other. A secret Auric now shared. "I like embroidering." In the immediacy of Lionel's death, when the nightmares had kept her awake, she would fix her energy on the attention it took her to complete a living scene upon the screen. Some of her more horrid pieces had kept her from the gasping, crying mess she so often was in those earlier days.

An inelegant, and wholly un-dukelike, snort escaped Auric, and just like that, he was the man she remembered and not the stern figure he presented to the *ton*.

"What?" she asked defensively, even as she warmed with the restored ease between them. "I do." To prove as much she pulled the needle through the fabric, releasing a relieved sigh as it sailed through the fabric and, this time, sparing her poor, wounded flesh.

"Since when do you embroider?" Auric looped his ankle over his knee.

Out the corner of her eyes, she stole a peek at him. "For some years now." Seven, to be precise. Not giving in to dark thoughts, she paused to arch an eyebrow. "I expect a lofty duke such as you would approve of a lady embroidering." And doing all manner of things dull.

Except, he refused to take the gentle bait she'd set out for him and so, with a little sigh, she returned her attention to the frame. Auric had always been such great fun to tease. He would tease back. They would smile. Now, he was always serious and somber and so very *dukish*.

The awkward silence stretched out between them, endless, until her skin burned from the impenetrable gaze he trained on her. She paused to steal another sideways glance and found him trying to make out the image on her frame, wholly uninterested in Daisy herself.

Invisible.

"What was that?" his low baritone cut into her thoughts.

A little shriek escaped her as she jammed the needle into her fingertip. "What was what?" She winced and popped the wounded digit into her mouth.

"You said something."

Daisy gave her head a firm shake and drew her finger out to assess the angry, red mark. "No, I didn't." Not intentionally, anyway. She'd developed the bothersome habit of talking to herself and creating horrible embroideries. "I daresay with you having not been to visit in some time," three weeks and six days, but really who was counting? "you've come 'round for a reason?" Her question, borderline rude, brought his eyebrows together. Then, powerful dukes such as he were likely unaccustomed to tart replies and annoyed young ladies.

"I always visit on Wednesdays."

"No," she corrected. Before he'd inherited the title of duke, a year after the death of Lionel, with a carriage accident that had claimed both his father and mother, he'd been a *very* different man. "No, you don't." He always *had* visited. This Season he'd devoted his attentions to duchess hunting—which is where his attention should be. Her lips pulled in a grimace. Well, not necessarily on finding a wife, but rather on himself and his own happiness. She'd never wanted to be a burden to him, never wanted to be an obligation.

It wasn't always that way . . .

Auric drummed his fingertips on the edge of his thigh and she followed the subtle movement. Her mouth went dry as she took in the thick, corded muscles encased in buff skin breeches. He really possessed quite splendid thighs. Not the legs one might expect of a duke. But rather—"You're displeased, Daisy."

His words jerked her from her improper musings. "What would I have to be displeased with?" Displeased would never be the right word. Regretful. Disappointed. For the years she'd spent waiting for him to see more where she was concerned, he continued to see nothing at all. To give her fingers something to do, Daisy drew the needle through the frame, working on her piece, all the while her skin pricked with the feel of being studied.

"What is it?"

She jerked her head up so swiftly, she wrenched the muscles of her neck. Daisy winced, resisting the urge to knead the tight flesh. "What is what?" She glanced about.

Auric nodded to her frame.

"This?" Oh, drat. Why must he be so blasted astute? She alternated her attention between his pointed stare and her embroidery frame then pulled it protectively to her chest.

His firm lips tugged with a nearly imperceptible hint of amusement. "Yes, what are you embroidering?"

Then knowing it would be futile to casually ignore his bold question, she turned the frame around. Even as she revealed her work, her cheeks warmed with embarrassment over her meager efforts.

"What is *that*?" His sharp bark of laughter caught her momentarily unawares. The sound emerged rusty, as if from ill use, but rich and full, nonetheless. She missed his laughter. She'd still rather it not be directed *her* way.

"Oh, hush." She jerked the frame back onto her lap. Then she glanced down eyeing the scrap. It really wasn't *that* bad. Or perhaps it was. After all, she'd spent several years trying to perfect this blasted image and could, herself, barely decipher the poor attempt. "What do you think it is?" She really was quite curious.

"I daresay I'd require another glance."

Daisy turned it back around and held it up for his inspection. Silence stretched on. Surely, he had some manner of guess? "Well?" she prodded.

"I'm still trying to make it out," he murmured as if to himself. Lines of consternation creased his brow. "A circle with a dip in the center?"

"Precisely." Precisely what she'd taken it as, anyway. Daisy tossed the frame atop the table, inadvertently rustling the gossip sheet and drawing Auric's attention from one embarrassment—to the next.

As bold as though he sat in his own parlor, he reached for the paper. With alacrity, Daisy swiped it off the table just as his fingers brushed the corner of the sheets. "You don't read gossip." She dropped it over her shoulder where it sailed to the floor in a noisy rustle. "Dukes don't read scandal sheets."

"And you have a good deal of experience with dukes, do you?" Amusement underscored his question.

She didn't have a good deal of experience with any gentlemen. "You're my only duke," she confided. Couldn't very well go mentioning her remarkable lack of insight with gentlemen.

His lips twitched again.

A servant rushed into the room bearing a silver tray of biscuits and tea, cutting into whatever he intended to say. The young woman set her burden on the table before them and dipped a curtsy, then backed out of the room. Daisy's maid, Agnes reentered and took a seat in the corner, with her own embroidery. The servant was far more impressive with a needle than Daisy could ever hope to be.

"How is your mother?"

Ah, of course. The reason for his visit. Auric, the Duke of Crawford, was the ever respectful, unfailingly polite gentleman.

"She is indisposed," she said with a deliberate vagueness. Only Auric truly understood the depth of her mother's misery and, even so, not the full extent of the woman's sorrow. Daisy would not draw him into her sad, sorry, little world. She reached for the porcelain teapot and steeped a delicate cup full, adding milk and three sugars. She ventured he had enough of his own sad, sorry, little world.

Auric accepted the fragile, porcelain cup. "Thank you," he murmured, taking a sip.

"Well, out with it." Daisy poured another, also with milk and three sugars. "After your absence, there must be a reason for your visit."

"Am I not permitted to call?"

She snorted. "You're a duke. I venture, you're permitted to do anything you want." Just so the new stodgier version of his younger self knew she jested, Daisy followed her words with a wink.

Daisy stared expectantly back at him.

Auric considered her question. *Why do I visit?* Repeatedly. Again and again. Week after week. Year after year.

The truth was guilt brought him back. It was a powerful sentiment that had held him in an unrelenting grip for seven years and he suspected always would. Selfishly, there were times he wished Daisy was invisible. But she wasn't. Nor would she ever be. No matter how much he willed it. "Come, Daisy," Auric took a sip and then provided the safe, polite answer. "I enjoy your company. Surely you know that."

She choked on her tea. "Why, that was a bit belated."

He frowned, not particularly caring to have the veracity of his words called into question—even if it was by a slip of a lady he'd known since she'd been a blubbering, babbling babe.

"I referred to your response," she clarified, unnecessarily. Then, like a governess praising her charge, Daisy leaned over and patted him on the knee. "It was still, however, very proper and polite."

"Are you questioning my sincerity?" Having known her since she'd been in the nursery, and he a boy of eight, there was nothing the least subservient or simpering about Daisy Meadows.

"Just a bit," she whispered and winked once more. Then a seriousness replaced the twinkle of mirth in her eyes. "I gather you've not come by because you're still nursing a broken heart over your Lady Anne." Lady Anne Adamson—or rather the former Lady Anne Adamson. Recently married to the roguish Earl of Stanhope, she'd now be referred to as the Countess of Stanhope in polite Society. The young lady also happened to be the woman he'd set his sights upon as his future duchess.

"A broken heart?" he scoffed. "I don't have a broken heart." He'd held the young lady in high regard. He found her to be a forthright woman who'd have him for more than his title, but there had been no love there. Daisy gave him a pointed look. "Regardless, what do you know of Lady Anne?"

"Come, Auric," she scoffed. "Just because I made my Come Out years ago and disappeared from your life doesn't mean I've not always worried after your happiness." At her directness, a twinge of guilt struck him. She'd always been a far better friend to him than he'd deserved. Daisy's initial entry into Society had been cut short by the untimely death of her father. She and her mother had retreated into mourning and had only reemerged this year.

He shifted in his seat, not at all comfortable discussing topics of his interest in another woman with Daisy. She was . . . was . . . well, *Daisy*. "I thought you didn't read the gossip columns?" he asked in attempt to steer the conversation away from matters of the heart.

"Ah, I said *you* didn't read the scandal sheets." She held up a finger and waved it about. "You're a duke, after all. I'm merely an unwed wallflower for which such pursuits are perfectly acceptable."

"You're n—"

"Yes, I am," she said simply, as though no more concerned with her marital state than she was with her rapidly cooling tea. "I'm very much a wallflower and quite content." She took a sip.

"Must you do that?" he groused, even as it was not at all dukelike to do something as common as grouse. She'd always had an uncanny ability to finish his thoughts, as he had hers. Still, it was quite unnerving when that skill was turned upon a person.

"Yes, there simply is no helping it. I'm afraid I'll have Season after Season until—"

"I referred to finishing my sentences."

Daisy set her teacup on the table in front of them and leaned forward, her palms pressed to her knees. "I know, Auric," she whispered as though imparting a great secret. "I was merely teasing. Though, I expect you're unaccustomed to people going about teasing you."

He took another sip and thought once more about the only lady who'd managed to capture his attention. The Lady Anne Adamson, now Countess of Stanhope. There had been nothing fawning about the lady, which had been some of the appeal to the now wedded woman.

Daisy patted his hand. "You are better served in her belonging to the earl. You'd not wed a woman who is in love with another."

A dull flush heated his neck at the intimate direction she'd
steered their discourse once more. Words of love and affection and hearts had no place between him and Daisy. Theirs
was a comfortable friendship borne of their families' connection and strengthened by a loss they shared. A friendship
that would likely not be if she learned the role he'd played
in her brother's death. She'd certainly not be smiling and
teasing him as she now did. Pain knifed at his chest. With
a forcible effort, he thrust back his dark, regretful thoughts.
"I've quite accepted Lady Anne's decision." There, that
was a vague enough response. He felt inclined to add,
"Nor was my heart fully engaged."

Daisy let out a beleaguered sigh. "If that was the romance
you reserved for the lady, it is no wonder she chose another."

Instead of rising to her baiting, he asked, "Are you a
romantic now, Daisy Meadows? Dreaming of love matches?"

"What should I dream of?" She sent a dark eyebrow
sweeping upward. "A cold, emotionless union to a gentleman who'd wed me for my dowry?"

Auric stilled and looked at the girl, Daisy, and conceded, in
this moment with talks of hearts and love matches and unions,
that she was no longer a girl, rather a woman. "You've always
been something of a romantic." A woman who, if one sorted
through her entrance, and disappearance, and then reemer-
gence into Society, was on her third Season, no less. She professed herself to be a wallflower. He eyed her a moment. He
took in the dark, curled hair piled atop her head, the shock of
freckles on her cheeks and nose, her too full mouth. Uniquely
different than the Incomparables, she'd never be considered
a great beauty by Society's rigid standards, and yet certainly
interesting enough to make a match with a proper gentleman.
"You desire love then, do you?" he asked, hating that it was

not Lionel here having this discussion with her—for so very many reasons.

Auric expected her to debate the charge. Instead, she again sighed and picked up her embroidery frame. "You always were entirely too practical." She paused. "And clever. You are indeed, correct. I'm a romantic." Daisy looked down a long moment at her embroidery frame and then turned the ambiguous needlepoint toward him. "You really cannot tell what it is?"

"No idea," he said succinctly. On the heel of that was a sudden, unexpected, and *unwelcome* possibility. "Has some gentleman captured your affections?" Whoever the blighter was, he was unworthy of her.

She paused, for the span of a heartbeat. "Don't be silly."

His shoulders sagged with relief. He didn't care to think of Daisy setting her affections on some gentleman because it would require Auric to take a role in determining that man's suitability as her match and he did not welcome that responsibility. Not yet. Oh, as she'd pointed out, with her out a second time, it was likely she'd need to make a match soon. However, it was not a prospect he relished. There was too much responsibility that went with seeing to her future. Auric finished his tea and set aside his cup. He tugged out his watch fob and consulted the timepiece attached.

"You have business?" she asked with a dryness to her tone that hinted at her having identified his eagerness to take his leave.

"Indeed," he murmured as he stood. "Will you give my regards to your mother and send her my apologies for not visiting in—?"

"Three weeks?" Daisy rose in a flurry of sea foam skirts, that silly embroidery in her hands. "I shall." With her chocolate brown gaze, she searched his face. For a moment she opened her mouth, as though she wished to say more but then closed it.

He sketched a bow and started for the door.

"Auric?"

Her quietly spoken question brought him to a stop and he froze at the threshold. He cast a questioning glance back over his shoulder.

Daisy folded her hands, one gloved, the other devoid of that proper garment. He eyed her fingers a moment; long, exposed, graceful. How had he failed to note what magnificent hands she possessed? With a hard shake of his head, he concentrated on the lady's words. "You needn't feel an obligation to us. You've responsibilities. My mother and I, we know that." A pressure tightened his chest. She held his gaze. "Lionel would have known that, too," she assured him, unknowingly squeezing the vise all the more, making breathing difficult.

The polite and, at the very least, gentlemanly thing to do was assure Daisy that his visit was more than an obligatory call. But that would be a lie. His debt to this family was great. He managed a jerky nod and swept from the room, feeling the familiar relief at each departure from the Marchioness of Roxbury's home awash in memories.

Auric strode down the long, carpeted corridors, past the oil canvas paintings of landscapes and bucolic, country scenes.

Except with the relief at having paid his requisite visit, there was guilt. A new niggling of guilt that didn't have to do with his failures the night Lionel had been killed, and everything do with the sudden, staggering truth that Daisy Meadows was on her third Season, unwed, and . . . he shuddered, romantic.

Bloody hell. The girl had grown up and he wanted as little do with Daisy dreaming of a love match as he did with a scheming matchmaking mama with designs upon his title. The pressure was too great to not err where she was concerned.

He reached the foyer. The late Marquess of Roxbury's devoted, white-haired butler stood in wait, Auric's black cloak in his hands. "Your carriage awaits, Your Grace." There was much to be said for a man who'd leave the employ of the man who inherited the title and remain on the more modest staff of the marchioness and her daughter.

"Thank you, Frederick," he murmured to the servant he'd known since his boyhood.

The man inclined his head as Auric shrugged into his cloak and then Auric hesitated. As a duke he enlisted the help of very few. He didn't go about making inquiries to servants, particularly other peoples' servants, and yet, this was the butler who'd demonstrated discretion with his and Lionel's every scheme through the years. A man who'd rejected the post of butler to the new Marquess of Roxbury following the other man's death and remained loyal to Daisy and her mother. "Tell me, Frederick, is there . . ." He flicked an imaginary piece of lint from his sleeve. "Has a certain gentleman captured Lady Daisy's attentions?"

"Beg pardon, Your Grace?"

"A gentleman." He made a show of adjusting his cloak. "More particularly an unworthy gentleman you," *I*, "would worry of where the lady is concerned?" A gentleman with dishonorable intentions, perhaps, or one of those bounders after her dowry, who'd take advantage of her whimsical hopes of love. He fisted his hands wanting to end the faceless, nameless, and still, as of now, *fictional* fiend.

Frederick lowered his voice. "Not an unworthy gentle-man, Your Grace. No."

Auric released a breath as the old servant rushed to pull open the door. Except as he strode down the handful of steps toward his waiting carriage, he glanced back at the closed door, a frown on his lips as the butler's words registered through his earlier relief.

Not an unworthy gentleman . . . Not. *No.* Not. *There is no gentleman who's captured the lady's affection.*

That suggested there was, in fact, a gentleman. And Daisy, with her silly romantic sentiments required more of a care-ful eye. "Bloody hell," he muttered as he climbed inside his carriage. He had an obligation to Lionel, and to Daisy, his friend's sister.

Whether he wished it or not.

Other Books by Christi Caldwell

Historical Romances

Lords of Honor Series
Seduced by a Lady's Heart
Captivated by a Lady's Charm
Rescued by a Lady's Love
Tempted by a Lady's Smile

Scandalous Seasons Series
Forever Betrothed, Never the Bride
Never Courted, Suddenly Wed
Always Proper, Suddenly Scandalous
Always a Rogue, Forever Her Love
A Marquess for Christmas
Once a Wallflower, at Last His Love

Sinful Brides Series
The Rogue's Wager
The Scoundrel's Honor

Standalones
'Twas the Night Before Scandal
The Theodosia Sword

Contemporary Romances

Danby Novellas
A Season of Hope
Winning a Lady's Heart

Acknowledgments

FOR MY MEME MASTER

Thank you for always finding my Chapter 22s.
And more importantly, thank you for being my friend!

About the Author

USA TODAY bestselling author Christi Caldwell blames Judith McNaught for luring her into the world of historical romance. While sitting in her graduate school apartment at the University of Connecticut, Christi decided to set aside her notes and pick up her laptop to try her hand at romance. She believes the most perfect heroes and heroines have imperfections, and she rather enjoys torturing them before crafting them a well-deserved happily ever after!

Christi makes her home in southern Connecticut, where she spends her time writing her own enchanting historical romances, chasing around her spirited son, and caring for her twin princesses in training!

Connect With Christi!

Christi's Website christicaldwell.com

Christi's Facebook Page https://www.facebook
.com/Christi-Caldwell-215250258658392/

Christi's Twitter Page
https://twitter.com/christicaldwell
@ChristiCaldwell

Christi's Amazon Profile https://www.amazon.com/
Christi-Caldwell/e/B0061UVSPO/
ref=sr_tc_2_0?qid=1483995621&sr=1-2-ent

Christi's Goodreads Profile
https://www.goodreads.com/author/show/
5297089.Christi_Caldwell

Subscribe to Christi's Newsletter
http://christicaldwellauthor
.authornewsletters.com/?p=subscribe&id=1

Contact Christi http://christicaldwell.com/contact

CPSIA information can be obtained
at www.ICGtesting.com
Printed in the USA
LVHW02s2128050618
579728LV00002B/2/P